CW00505321

# George Farquhar

# The Inconstant

**George Farquhar**

# The Inconstant

1st Edition | ISBN: 978-3-75238-221-1

Place of Publication: Frankfurt am Main, Germany

Year of Publication: 2020

Outlook Verlag GmbH, Germany.

Reproduction of the original.

THE

# INCONSTANT
## By GEORGE FARQUHAR

# REMARKS.

This comedy, by a favourite writer, had a reception, on the first night of its appearance, far inferior to that of his other productions. It was, with difficulty, saved from condemnation; and the author, in his preface, has boldly charged some secret enemies with having attempted its destruction.

Dramatic authors have fewer enemies at the present period, or they have more humility, than formerly. For now, when their works are hissed from the stage, they acknowledge they have had a fair trial, and deserve their fate. Wherefore should an author seek for remote causes, to account for his failures, when to himself alone, he is certain ever to impute all his success?

Neither the wit, humour, nor the imitation of nature, in this play, are of that forcible kind, with which the audience had been usually delighted by Farquhar; and, that the moral gave a degree of superiority to this drama, was, in those days, of little consequence: the theatre was ordained, it was thought, for mere pleasure, nor did any one wish it should degenerate into instruction.

It may be consolatory to the disappointed authors of the present day, to find, how the celebrated author of this comedy was incommoded with theatrical crosses. He was highly offended, that his play was not admired; still more angry, that there was an empty house, on his sixth night, and more angry still, that the Opera House, for the benefit of a French dancer, was, about this time, filled even to the annoyance of the crowded company. The following are his own words on the occasion:

"It is the prettiest way in the world of despising the French king, to let him see that we can afford money to bribe his dancers, when he, poor man, has exhausted all his stock, in buying some pitiful towns and principalities. What can be a greater compliment to our generous nation, than to have the lady on her re-tour to Paris, boast of her splendid entertainment in England: of the complaisance, liberty, and good nature of a people, who thronged her house so full, that she had not room to stick a pin; and left a poor fellow, who had the misfortune of being one of themselves, without one farthing, for half a year's pains he had taken for their entertainment."

This complaint is curious, on account of the talents of the man who makes it; and, for the same cause, highly reprehensible. If Farquhar, thought himself superior to the French dancer, why did he honour her by a comparison? and, if he wanted bread, why did he not suffer in silence, rather than insinuate, he should like to receive it, through the medium of a benefit?

A hundred years of refinement (the exact time since this author wrote) may have weakened the force of the dramatic pen; but it has, happily, elevated authors above the servile spirit of dedications, or the meaner practice, of taking public benefits.

As the moral of this comedy has been mentioned as one of its highest recommendations, it must be added—that, herein, the author did not invent, but merely adopt, as his own, an occurrence which took place in Paris, about that period, just as he has represented it in his last act. The Chevalier de Chastillon was the man who is personated by young Mirabel, in this extraordinary event; and the Chevalier's friend, his betrothed wife, and his beautiful courtesan, are all exactly described in the characters of Duretete, Oriana, and Lamorce.

Having justly abridged Farquhar of the honour of inventing a moral, it may be equally just, to make a slight apology for his chagrin at the slender receipts of his sixth night.—He once possessed the income, which arose from a captain's commission in the army; and having prudently conceived that this little revenue would not maintain a wife, he had resolved to live single, unless chance should bestow on him a woman of fortune. His person and address were so extremely alluring, that a woman of family, but of no fortune, conceiving the passion she felt for him to be love, pretended she possessed wealth, and deceived him into a marriage, which plunged them both into the utmost poverty.

This admirable dramatist seems to have been born for a dupe. In his matrimonial distress, he applied to a nobleman, who had professed a friendship for him, and besought his advice how to surmount his difficulties: The counsel given, was—"Sell your commission, for present support, and, before the money for its sale is expended, I will procure you another." Farquhar complied—and his patron broke his word.

---

## DRAMATIS PERSONÆ.

| | |
|---|---|
| OLD MIRABEL | *Mr. Dowton.* |
| YOUNG MIRABEL | *Mr. C. Kemble.* |

| | |
|---|---|
| CAPTAIN DURETETE | *Mr. Bannister.* |
| DUGARD | *Mr. Holland.* |
| PETIT | *Mr. De Camp.* |

BRAVOES—*Messrs. Maddocks, Webb, Evans and Sparks.*

| | |
|---|---|
| ORIANA | *Mrs. Young.* |
| BISARRE | *Mrs. Jordan.* |
| LAMORCE | *Miss Tidswell.* |

**THE**

# INCONSTANT.

---

## ACT THE FIRST.

### SCENE I.

*The Street.*

*Enter* DUGARD, *and his Man,* PETIT, *in Riding Habits.*

*Dug.* Sirrah, what's o'clock?

*Petit.* Turned of eleven, sir.

*Dug.* No more! We have rid a swinging pace from Nemours, since two this morning! Petit, run to Rousseau's, and bespeak a dinner, at a Lewis d'or a head, to be ready by one.

*Petit.* How many will there be of you, sir?

*Dug.* Let me see—Mirabel one, Duretete two, myself three——

*Petit.* And I four.

*Dug.* How now, sir? at your old travelling familiarity! When abroad, you had some freedom, for want of better company, but among my friends, at Paris, pray remember your distance —Begone, sir! [*Exit* PETIT.] This fellow's wit was necessary abroad, but he's too cunning for a domestic; I must dispose of him some way else.—Who's here? Old Mirabel, and my sister!—my dearest sister!

*Enter* OLD MIRABEL *and* ORIANA.

*Oriana.* My Brother! Welcome!

*Dug.* Monsieur Mirabel! I'm heartily glad to see you.

*Old Mir.* Honest Mr. Dugard, by the blood of the Mirabels, I'm your most humble servant!

*Dug.* Why, sir, you've cast your skin, sure; you're brisk and gay—lusty health about you—no sign of age, but your silver hairs.

*Old Mir.* Silver hairs! Then they are quicksilver hairs, sir. Whilst I have golden pockets, let my hairs be silver, an' they will. Adsbud, sir, I can dance, and sing, and drink, and—no, I can't wench. But Mr. Dugard, no news of my son Bob in all your travels?

*Dug.* Your son's come home, sir.

*Old Mir.* Come home! Bob come home! By the blood of the Mirabels, Mr. Dugard, what say you?

*Oriana.* Mr. Mirabel returned, sir?

*Dug.* He's certainly come, and you may see him within this hour or two.

*Old Mir.* Swear it, Mr. Dugard, presently swear it.

*Dug.* Sir, he came to town with me this morning; I left him at the Banieurs, being a little disordered after riding, and I shall see him again presently.

*Old Mir.* What! and he was ashamed to ask a blessing with his boots on! A nice dog! Well, and how fares the young rogue, ha?

*Dug.* A fine gentleman, sir; he'll be his own messenger.

*Old Mir.* A fine gentleman! But is the rogue like me still?

*Dug.* Why, yes, sir; he's very like his mother, and as like you, as most modern sons are to their fathers.

*Old Mir.* Why, sir, don't you think that I begat him?

*Dug.* Why, yes, sir; you married his mother, and he inherits your estate. He's very like you, upon my word.

*Oriana.* And pray, brother, what's become of his honest

6

companion, Duretete?

*Dug.* Who, the captain? The very same, he went abroad; he's the only Frenchman I ever knew, that could not change. Your son, Mr. Mirabel, is more obliged to nature for that fellow's composition, than for his own: for he's more happy in Duretete's folly than his own wit. In short, they are as inseparable as finger and thumb; but the first instance in the world, I believe, of opposition in friendship.

*Old Mir.* Very well: will he be home, to dinner, think ye?

*Dug.* Sir, he has ordered me to bespeak a dinner for us at Rousseau's, at a Lewis d'or a head.

*Old Mir.* A Lewis d'or a head! Well said, Bob; by the blood of the Mirabels, Bob's improved! But, Mr. Dugard, was it so civil of Bob, to visit Monsieur Rousseau, before his own natural father, eh? Harkye, Oriana, what think you now, of a fellow that can eat and drink ye a whole Lewis d'or at a sitting? He must be as strong as Hercules; life and spirit in abundance. Before Gad, I don't wonder at these men of quality, that their own wives can't serve them! A Lewis d'or a head! 'tis enough to stock the whole nation with bastards, 'tis, 'faith! Mr. Dugard, I leave you with your sister.[*Exit.*

*Dug.* Well, sister, I need not ask you how you do, your looks resolve me; fair, tall, well-shaped; you're almost grown out of my remembrance.

*Oriana.* Why, truly, brother, I look pretty well, thank nature, and my toilet; I eat three meals a day, am very merry when up, and sleep soundly when I'm down.

*Dug.* But, sister, you remember that upon my going abroad, you would chuse this old gentleman for your guardian; he's no more related to our family, than Prester John, and I have no reason to think you mistrusted my management of your fortune. Therefore, pray be so kind as to tell me, without reservation, the true cause of making such a choice.

*Oriana.* Lookye, brother, you were going a rambling, and 'twas proper, lest I should go a rambling too, that somebody should take care of me. Old Monsieur Mirabel is an honest gentleman, was our father's friend, and has a young lady in his house, whose company I like, and who has chosen him for her guardian as well as I.

*Dug.* Who, Mademoiselle Bisarre?

*Oriana.* The same; we live merrily together, without scandal or reproach; we make much of the old gentleman between us, and he takes care of us; all the week we dance and sing, and upon Sundays, go first to church, and then to the play.—Now, brother, besides these motives for chusing this gentleman for my guardian, perhaps I had some private reasons.

*Dug.* Not so private as you imagine, sister; your love to young Mirabel's no secret, I can assure you, but so public, that all your friends are ashamed on't.

*Oriana.* O' my word, then, my friends are very bashful; though I'm afraid, sir, that those people are not ashamed enough at their own crimes, who have so many blushes to spare for the faults of their neighbours.

*Dug.* Ay, but, sister, the people say——

*Oriana.* Pshaw! hang the people! they'll talk treason, and profane their Maker; must we, therefore infer, that our king is a tyrant, and religion a cheat? Lookye, brother, their court of inquiry is a tavern, and their informer, claret: They think as they drink, and swallow reputations like loches; a lady's health goes briskly round with the glass, but her honour is lost in the toast.

*Dug.* Ay, but sister, there is still something——

*Oriana.* If there be something, brother, 'tis none of the people's something: Marriage is my thing, and I'll stick to't.

*Dug.* Marriage! young Mirabel marry! he'll build churches sooner. Take heed, sister, though your honour stood proof to his home-bred assaults, you must keep a stricter guard for the future: He has now got the foreign air, and the Italian softness; his wit's improved by converse, his behaviour finished by observation, and his assurances confirmed by success. Sister, I can assure you, he has made his conquests; and 'tis a plague upon your sex, to be the soonest deceived, by those very men that you know have been false to others.—But then, sister, he's as fickle—

*Oriana.* For God's sake, brother, tell me no more of his faults, for, if you do, I shall run mad for him: Say no more, sir; let me but get him into the bands of matrimony, I'll spoil his wandering, I warrant him; I'll do his business that way, never fear.

*Dug.* Well, sister, I won't pretend to understand the engagements between you and your lover; I expect when you have need of my counsel or assistance, you will let me know more of your affairs. Mirabel is a gentleman, and as far as my honour and interest can reach, you may command me, to the furtherance of your happiness: In the mean time, sister, I have a great mind to make you a present of another humble servant; a fellow that I took up at Lyons, who has served me honestly ever since.

*Oriana.* Then why will you part with him?

*Dug.* He has gained so insufferably on my good-humour, that he's grown too familiar; but the fellow's cunning, and may be serviceable to you in your affair with Mirabel. Here he comes.

*Enter* PETIT.

Well, sir, have you been at Rousseau's?

*Petit.* Yes, sir, and who should I find there but Mr. Mirabel and the captain, hatching as warmly over a tub of ice, as two hen pheasants over a brood—They would not let me bespeak any thing, for they had dined before I came.

*Dug.* Come, sir, you shall serve my sister, I shall still continue kind to you; and if your lady recommends your diligence, upon trial, I'll use my interest to advance you.— Wait on your lady home, Petit.[*Exit.*

*Petit.* A chair! a chair! a chair!

*Oriana.* No, no, I'll walk home, 'tis but next door.[*Exeunt.*

## SCENE II.

*A Tavern.*

Young Mirabel *and* Duretete *discovered, rising from Table.*

*Y. Mir.* Welcome to Paris once more, my dear Captain; we have eat heartily, drank roundly, paid plentifully, and let it go for once. I liked every thing but our women; they looked so lean and tawdry, poor creatures! 'Tis a sure sign the army is not paid. Give me the plump Venetian, brisk, and sanguine, that smiles upon me like the glowing sun, and meets my lips like sparkling wine, her person, shining as the glass, and spirit, like the foaming liquor.

*Dur.* Ah, Mirabel, Italy I grant you; but for our women here in France, they are such thin, brawn, fallen jades, a man may as well make a bed-fellow of a cane chair.

*Y. Mir.* France! A light, unseasoned country, nothing but feathers, foppery, and fashions.—There's nothing on this side the Alps worth my humble service t'ye—Ha, Roma la Santa! —Italy for my money!—their customs, gardens, buildings, paintings, music, policies, wine, and women! the paradise of the world!—not pestered with a parcel of precise, old, gouty fellows, that would debar their children every pleasure, that they themselves are past the sense of;—commend me to the Italian familiarity—"Here, son, there's fifty crowns, go, pay your girl her week's allowance."

*Dur.* Ay, these are your fathers, for you, that understand the necessities of young men! not like our musty dads, who, because they cannot fish themselves, would muddy the water, and spoil the sport of them that can. But now you talk of the plump, what d'ye think of a Dutch woman?

*Y. Mir.* A Dutch woman's too compact,—nay, every thing among them is so; a Dutch man is thick, a Dutch woman is squab, a Dutch horse is round, a Dutch dog is short, a Dutch ship is broad bottomed; and, in short, one would swear, that the whole product of the country were cast in the same mould with their cheeses.

*Dur.* Ay, but Mirabel, you have forgot the English ladies.

*Y. Mir.* The women of England were excellent, did they not take such unsufferable pains to ruin, what nature has made so incomparably well; they would be delicate creatures indeed, could they but thoroughly arrive at the French mien, or entirely let it alone; for they only spoil a very good air of their own, by an awkward imitation of ours. But come, Duretete, let us mind the business in hand; Mistresses we must have, and must take up with the manufacture of the place, and upon a competent diligence, we shall find those in Paris shall match the Italians from top to toe.

*Dur.* Ay, Mirabel, you will do well enough, but what will become of your friend? you know, I am so plaguy bashful! so naturally an ass upon these occasions, that——

*Y. Mir.* Pshaw! you must be bolder, man! Travel three years, and bring home such a baby as bashfulness! A great lusty fellow, and a soldier; fie upon it!

*Dur.* Lookye, sir, I can visit, and I can ogle a little,—as thus, or thus now. Then I can kiss abundantly—but if they chance to give me a forbidding look, as some women, you know, have a devilish cast with their eyes—or if they cry, "What do you mean? what d'ye take me for? Fie, sir, remember who I am, sir—A person of quality to be used at this rate!"—'Egad, I'm struck as flat as a fryingpan.

*Y. Mir.* Words of course! never mind them: Turn you about upon your heel, with a jantée air; hum out the end of an old song; cut a cross caper, and at her again.

*Dur.* [*Imitates him.*] No, hang it, 'twill never do!—Oons! what did my father mean, by sticking me up in an university, or to think that I should gain any thing by my head, in a nation, whose genius lies all in their heels!—Well, if ever I come to have children of my own, they shall have the education of the country—they shall learn to dance, before they can walk, and be taught to sing, before they can speak.

*Y. Mir.* Come, come, throw off that childish humour—put on assurance, there's no avoiding it; stand all hazards, thou'rt a stout, lusty fellow, and hast a good estate;—look bluff, hector, you have a good side-box face, a pretty impudent face; so, that's pretty well.—This fellow went abroad like an ox, and is returned like an ass.[*Aside.*

*Dur.* Let me see now, how I look. [*Pulls out a Pocket Glass, and looks on it.*] A side-box face, say you!—'Egad, I don't like it, Mirabel! Fie, sir, don't abuse your friends, I could not wear such a face for the best countess in christendom.

*Y. Mir.* Why can't you, blockhead, as well as I?

*Dur.* Why, thou hast impudence to set a good face upon any thing; I would change half my gold for half thy brass, with all my heart. Who comes here? Odso, Mirabel, your father!

*Enter* OLD MIRABEL.

*Old Mir.* Where's Bob?—dear Bob?

*Y. Mir.* Your blessing, sir?

*Old Mir.* My blessing! Damn ye, ye young rogue, why did not you come to see your father first, sirrah? My dear boy, I am heartily glad to see thee, my dear child, 'faith!—Captain Duretete, by the blood of the Mirabels, I'm yours! Well, my lads, ye look bravely, 'faith.—Bob, hast got any money left?

*Y. Mir.* Not a farthing, sir.

*Old Mir.* Why, then, I won't gi' thee a souse.

*Y. Mir.* I did but jest, here's ten pistoles.

*Old Mir.* Why, then, here's ten more: I love to be charitable to those that don't want it.—Well, and how do you like Italy, my boys?

*Y. Mir.* O, the garden of the world, sir! Rome, Naples, Venice, Milan, and a thousand others—all fine.

*Old Mir.* Ay! say you so? And they say, that Chiari is very fine too.

*Dur.* Indifferent, sir, very indifferent; a very scurvy air, the most unwholesome to a French constitution in the world.

*Y. Mir.* Pshaw! nothing on't: these rascally gazetteers have misinformed you.

*Old Mir.* Misinformed me! Oons, sir, were we not beaten

12

there?

*Y. Mir.* Beaten, sir! we beaten!

*Old Mir.* Why, how was it, pray, sweet sir?

*Y. Mir.* Sir, the captain will tell you.

*Dur.* No, sir, your son will tell you.

*Y. Mir.* The captain was in the action, sir.

*Dur.* Your son saw more than I, sir, for he was a looker on.

*Old Mir.* Confound you both, for a brace of cowards! here are no Germans to overhear you—why don't ye tell me how it was?

*Y. Mir.* Why, then, you must know, that we marched up a body of the finest, bravest, well dressed fellows in the universe; our commanders at the head of us, all lace and feather, like so many beaux at a ball—I don't believe there was a man of them but could dance a charmer, Morbleau.

*Old Mir.* Dance! very well, pretty fellows, 'faith!

*Y. Mir.* We capered up to their very trenches, and there saw, peeping over, a parcel of scare-crow, olive-coloured, gunpowder fellows, as ugly as the devil.

*Dur.* E'gad, I shall never forget the looks of them, while I have breath to fetch.

*Y. Mir.* They were so civil, indeed, as to welcome us with their cannon! but for the rest, we found them such unmannerly, rude, unsociable dogs, that we grew tired of their company, and so we e'en danced back again.

*Old Mir.* And did ye all come back?

*Y. Mir.* No, two or three thousand of us staid behind.

*Old Mir.* Why, Bob, why?

*Y. Mir.* Pshaw! because they could not come that night.

*Dur.* No, sir, because they could not come that night.

*Y. Mir.* But, come, sir, we were talking of something else; pray, how does your lovely charge, the fair Oriana?

*Old Mir.* Ripe, sir, just ripe; you'll find it better engaging with her than with the Germans, let me tell you. And what would you say, my young Mars, if I had a Venus for thee too? Come, Bob, your apartment is ready, and pray let your friend be my guest too; you shall command the house between ye, and I'll be as merry as the best of you.[*Exeunt.*

## ACT THE SECOND.

### SCENE I.

OLD MIRABEL'S *House.*

ORIANA *and* BISARRE.

*Bis.* And you love this young rake, d'ye?

*Oriana.* Yes.

*Bis.* In spite of all his ill usage?

*Oriana.* I can't help it.

*Bis.* What's the matter wi' ye?

*Oriana.* Pshaw!

*Bis.* Um!—before that any young, lying, swearing, flattering, rakehelly fellow, should play such tricks with me— O, the devil take all your Cassandras and Cleopatras for me.— I warrant now, you'll play the fool when he comes, and say you love him! eh?

*Oriana.* Most certainly; I can't dissemble, Bisarre; besides, 'tis past that, we're contracted.

*Bis.* Contracted! alack-a-day, poor thing!—What, you have changed rings, or broken an old broadpiece between you! I would make a fool of any fellow in France. Well, I must confess, I do love a little coquetting, with all my heart! my business should be to break gold with my lover one hour, and crack my promise the next; he should find me one day with a prayer book in my hand, and with a play book another.—He should have my consent to buy the wedding ring, and the next moment would I ask him his name.

*Oriana.* O, my dear! were there no greater tie upon my heart, than there is upon my conscience, I would soon throw the contract out of doors; but the mischief on't is, I am so fond of being tied, that I'm forced to be just, and the strength of my passion keeps down the inclination of my sex.

*Bis.* But here's the old gentleman!

*Enter* OLD MIRABEL.

*Old Mir.* Where's my wenches?—where's my two little girls? Eh! Have a care,—look to yourselves, 'faith, they're a coming—the travellers are a coming! Well! which of you two will be my daughter-in-law now? Bisarre, Bisarre, what say you, madcap? Mirabel is a pure, wild fellow.

*Bis.* I like him the worse.

*Old Mir.* You lie, hussy, you like him the better, indeed you do! What say you, my t'other little filbert, eh?

*Oriana.* I suppose the gentleman will chuse for himself, sir.

*Old Mir.* Why, that's discreetly said, and so he shall.

*Enter* MIRABEL *and* DURETETE; *they salute the Ladies.*

Bob, harkye, you shall marry one of these girls, sirrah!

*Y. Mir.* Sir, I'll marry them both, if you please.

*Bis.* [*Aside.*] He'll find that one may serve his turn.

*Old Mir.* Both! why, you young dog, d'ye banter me?—Come, sir, take your choice.—Duretete, you shall have your choice too, but Robin shall chuse first.—Come, sir, begin. Well! which d'ye like?

*Y. Mir.* Both.

*Old Mir.* But which will you marry?

*Y. Mir.* Neither.

*Old Mir.* Neither! Don't make me angry now, Bob—pray, don't make me angry.—Lookye, sirrah, if I don't dance at your wedding to-morrow, I shall be very glad to cry at your grave.

*Y. Mir.* That's a bull, father.

*Old Mir.* A bull! Why, how now, ungrateful sir, did I make thee a man, that thou shouldst make me a beast?

*Y. Mir.* Your pardon, sir; I only meant your expression.

*Old Mir.* Harkye, Bob, learn better manners to your father before strangers! I won't be angry this time: But oons, if ever you do't again, you rascal!—remember what I say.[*Exit.*

*Y. Mir.* Pshaw! what does the old fellow mean by mewing me up here with a couple of green girls?—Come, Duretete, will you go?

*Oriana.* I hope, Mr. Mirabel, you han't forgot—

*Y. Mir.* No, no, madam, I han't forgot, I have brought you a thousand little Italian curiosities; I'll assure you, madam, as far as a hundred pistoles would reach, I han't forgot the least circumstance.

*Oriana.* Sir, you misunderstand me.

*Y. Mir.* Odso! the relics, madam, from Rome. I do remember, now, you made a vow of chastity before my departure; a vow of chastity, or something like it—was it not, madam?

*Oriana.* O sir, I'm answered at present.[*Exit.*

*Y. Mir.* She was coming full mouth upon me with her contract—'Would I might despatch t'other!

*Dur.* Mirabel, that lady there, observe her, she's wondrous pretty, 'faith! and seems to have but few words; I like her mainly—speak to her, man, pr'ythee speak to her.

*Y. Mir.* Madam, here's a gentleman, who declares——

*Dur.* Madam, don't believe him, I declare nothing—What, the devil, do you mean, man?

16

*Y. Mir.* He says, madam, that you are as beautiful as an angel.

*Dur.* He tells a damned lie, madam! I say no such thing— Are you mad, Mirabel? Why, I shall drop down with shame.

*Y. Mir.* And so, madam, not doubting but your ladyship may like him as well as he does you, I think it proper to leave you together.

[Going, D<small>URETETE</small> holds him.

*Dur.* Hold, hold—Why, Mirabel, friend, sure you won't be so barbarous as to leave me alone! Pr'ythee, speak to her for yourself, as it were! Lord, Lord, that a Frenchman should want impudence!

*Y. Mir.* You look mighty demure, madam.—She's deaf, Captain.

*Dur.* I had much rather have her dumb.

*Y. Mir.* The gravity of your air, madam, promises some extraordinary fruits from your study, which moves us with curiosity to inquire the subject of your ladyship's contemplation.—Not a word!

*Dur.* I hope in the Lord, she's speechless! if she be, she's mine this moment. Mirabel, d'ye think a woman's silence can be natural?

*Bis.* But the forms which logicians introduce, and which proceed from simple enumeration, are dubitable, and proceed only upon admittance—

*Y. Mir.* Hoyty toyty! what a plague have we here? Plato in petticoats!

*Dur.* Ay, ay, let her go on, man; she talks in my own mother tongue.

*Bis.* 'Tis exposed to invalidity, from a contradictory instance; looks only upon common operations, and is infinite in its termination.

*Y. Mir.* Rare pedantry!

*Dur.* Axioms! axioms! self-evident principles!

*Bis.* Then the ideas wherewith the mind is pre-occupate.— O, gentlemen, I hope you'll pardon my cogitation! I was involved in a profound point of philosophy, but I shall discuss it somewhere else, being satisfied, that the subject is not agreeable to your sparks, that profess the vanity of the times. [*Exit.*

*Y. Mir.* Go thy way, good wife Bias! Do you hear, Duretete? Dost hear this starched piece of austerity?

*Dur.* She's mine, man, she's mine—My own talent to a T.— I'll match her in dialectics, 'faith! I was seven years at the university, man, nursed up with Barbaro, Celarunt, Darii, Ferio, Baralipton. Did you ever know, man, that 'twas metaphysics made me an ass? It was, 'faith! Had she talked a word of singing, dancing, plays, fashions, or the like, I had foundered at the first step; but as she is—Mirabel, wish me joy!

*Y. Mir.* You don't mean marriage, I hope?

*Dur.* No, no, I am a man of more honour.

*Y. Mir.* Bravely resolved, Captain! now for thy credit—warm me this frozen snowball—'twill be a conquest above the Alps!

*Dur.* But will you promise to be always near me?

*Y. Mir.* Upon all occasions, never fear.

*Dur.* Why, then, you shall see me, in two moments, make an induction from my love to her hand, from her hand to her mouth, from her mouth to her heart, and so conclude in her bed, categorematice.

*Y. Mir.* Now the game begins, and my fool is entered.—But here comes one to spoil my sport; now shall I be teased to death, with this old-fashioned contract! I should love her too, if I might do it my own way, but she'll do nothing without witnesses, forsooth! I wonder women can be so immodest!

*Enter* ORIANA.

Well, madam, why d'ye follow me?

*Oriana.* Well, sir, why do you shun me?

*Y. Mir.* 'Tis my humour, madam, and I'm naturally swayed

18

by inclination.

*Oriana.* Have you forgot our contract, sir?

*Y. Mir.* All I remember of that contract is, that it was made some three years ago, and that's enough, in conscience, to forget the rest on't.

*Oriana.* 'Tis sufficient, sir, to recollect the passing of it; for, in that circumstance, I presume, lies the force of the obligation.

*Y. Mir.* Obligations, madam, that are forced upon the will, are no tie upon the conscience; I was a slave to my passion, when I passed the instrument, but the recovery of my freedom makes the contract void.

*Oriana.* Come, Mr. Mirabel, these expressions I expected from the raillery of your humour, but I hope for very different sentiments from your honour and generosity.

*Y. Mir.* Lookye, madam, as for my generosity, 'tis at your service, with all my heart: I'll keep you a coach and six horses, if you please, only permit me to keep my honour to myself. Consider, madam, you have no such thing among ye, and 'tis a main point of policy to keep no faith with reprobates —thou art a pretty little reprobate, and so get thee about thy business!

*Oriana.* Well, sir, even all this I will allow to the gaiety of your temper; your travels have improved your talent of talking, but they are not of force, I hope, to impair your morals.

*Y. Mir.* Morals! why, there 'tis again now!—I tell thee, child, there is not the least occasion for morals, in any business between you and I. Don't you know that, of all commerce in the world, there is no such cozenage and deceit, as in the traffic between man and woman? we study all our lives long, how to put tricks upon one another.—No fowler lays abroad more nets for his game, nor a hunter for his prey, than you do, to catch poor innocent men.—Why do you sit three or four hours at your toilet in a morning? only with a villanous design to make some poor fellow a fool before night. What d'ye sigh for?—What d'ye weep for?—What d'ye pray for? Why, for a husband: That is, you implore Providence to assist you, in the just, and pious design, of making the wisest of his creatures a fool, and the head of the creation, a slave.

*Oriana.* Sir, I am proud of my power, and am resolved to use it.

*Y. Mir.* Hold, hold, madam, not so fast—As you have variety of vanities to make coxcombs of us; so we have vows, oaths, and protestations, of all sorts and sizes, to make fools of you —And this, in short, my dear creature, is our present condition. I have sworn, and lied, briskly, to gain my ends of you; your ladyship has patched and painted violently, to gain your ends of me; but, since we are both disappointed, let us make a drawn battle, and part clear on both sides.

*Oriana.* With all my heart, sir! give me up my contract, and I'll never see your face again.

*Y. Mir.* Indeed, I won't, child!

*Oriana.* What, sir! neither do one nor t'other?

*Y. Mir.* No, you shall die a maid, unless you please to be otherwise, upon my terms.

*Oriana.* What do you intend by this, sir?

*Y. Mir.* Why, to starve you into compliance;—lookye, you shall never marry any man; and you had as good let me do you a kindness as a stranger.

*Oriana.* Sir, you're a——

*Y. Mir.* What am I, ma'am?

*Oriana.* A villain, sir.

*Y. Mir.* I'm glad on't—I never knew an honest fellow in my life, but was a villain upon these occasions. Han't you drawn yourself, now, into a very pretty dilemma? ha! ha! ha! the poor lady has made a vow of virginity, when she thought of making a vow to the contrary. Was ever poor woman so cheated into chastity?

*Oriana.* Sir, my fortune is equal to yours, my friends as powerful, and both shall be put to the test, to do me justice.

*Y. Mir.* What! you'll force me to marry you, will ye?

*Oriana.* Sir, the law shall.

*Y. Mir.* But the law can't force me to do any thing else, can it?

*Oriana.* Pshaw, I despise thee—Monster!

*Y. Mir.* Kiss and be friends, then—Don't cry, child, and you shall have your sugar plumb—Come, madam, d'ye think I could be so unreasonable as to make you fast all your life long! No, I did but jest, you shall have your liberty—here, take your contract, and give me mine.

*Oriana.* No, I won't.

*Y. Mir.* Eh! What, is the girl a fool?

*Oriana.* No, sir, you shall find me cunning enough to do myself justice; and since I must not depend upon your love, I'll be revenged, and force you to marry me, out of spite.

*Y. Mir.* Then I'll beat thee out of spite, and make a most confounded husband!

*Oriana.* O, sir, I shall match ye! A good husband makes a good wife at any time.

*Y. Mir.* I'll rattle down your china about your ears.

*Oriana.* And I'll rattle about the city, to run you in debt for more.

*Y. Mir.* I'll tear the furbelow off your clothes, and when you swoon for vexation, you shan't have a penny, to buy a bottle of hartshorn.

*Oriana.* And you, sir, shall have hartshorn in abundance.

*Y. Mir.* I'll keep as many mistresses as I have coach horses.

*Oriana.* And I'll keep as many gallants as you have grooms.

*Y. Mir.* But, sweet madam, there is such a thing as a divorce!

*Oriana.* But, sweet sir, there is such a thing as alimony! so divorce on, and spare not.[*Exit.*

*Y. Mir.* Ay, that separate maintenance is the devil—there's their refuge!—O' my conscience, one would take cuckoldom for a meritorious action, because the women are so handsomely rewarded for it.[*Exit.*

Enter D<small>URETETE</small> *and* P<small>ETIT</small>.

*Dur.* And she's mighty peevish, you say?

*Petit.* O sir, she has a tongue as long as my leg, and talks so crabbedly, you would think she always spoke Welsh.

*Dur.* That's an odd language, methinks, for her philosophy.

*Petit.* But sometimes she will sit you half a day without speaking a word, and talk oracles all the while by the wrinkles of her forehead, and the motions of her eyebrows.

*Dur.* Nay, I shall match her in philosophical ogles, 'faith!— that's my talent: I can talk best, you must know, when I say nothing.

*Petit.* But d'ye ever laugh, sir?

*Dur.* Laugh? Won't she endure laughing?

*Petit.* Why, she's a critic, sir, she hates a jest, for fear it should please her; and nothing keeps her in humour, but what gives her the spleen.—And then, for logic, and all that, you know——

*Dur.* Ay, ay, I'm prepared, I have been practising hard words and no sense, this hour, to entertain her.

*Petit.* Then place yourself behind this screen, that you may have a view of her behaviour before you begin.

*Dur.* I long to engage her, lest I should forget my lesson.

*Petit.* Here she comes, sir—I must fly.

[*Exit* P<small>ETIT</small>, *and* D<small>URETETE</small> *stands peeping<br>behind the Curtain.

Enter B<small>ISARRE</small> *and* M<small>AID</small>.

*Bis.* [*With a Book.*] Pshaw! hang books! they sour our temper, spoil our eyes, and ruin our complexions.

[*Throws away the Book.*

22

*Dur.* Eh? the devil such a word there is in all Aristotle!

*Bis.* Come, wench, let's be free—call in the fiddle, there's nobody near us.

*Dur.* 'Would to the Lord there was not!

*Bis.* Here, friend, a minuet——[*Music.*] Quicker time—ha—'would we had a man or two!

*Dur.* [*Stealing away.*] You shall have the devil sooner, my dear, dancing philosopher!

*Bis.* Uds my life!—Here's one!

> [*Runs to* DURETETE, *and hales him back.*

*Dur.* Is all my learned preparation come to this?

*Bis.* Come, sir, don't be ashamed, that's my good boy—you're very welcome, we wanted such a one—Come, strike up—[*Dance.*] I know you dance well, sir, you're finely shaped for't—Come, come, sir;—quick, quick! you miss the time else.

*Dur.* But, madam, I come to talk with you.

*Bis.* Ay, ay, talk as you dance, talk as you dance,—come.

*Dur.* But we were talking of dialectics—

*Bis.* Hang dialectics! [*Music.*] Mind the time——quicker, sirrah!—Come—and how d'ye find yourself now, sir?

*Dur.* In a fine breathing sweat, Doctor.

*Bis.* All the better, patient, all the better;—Come, sir, sing now, sing, I know you sing well: I see you have a singing face—a heavy, dull, sonata face.

*Dur.* Who, I sing?

*Bis.* O you're modest, sir—but come, sit down closer—closer. Here, a bottle of wine! [*Exit* MAID, *and returns with Wine.*] Come, sir—sing, sir.

*Dur.* But, madam, I came to talk with you.

*Bis.* O sir, you shall drink first.—Come, fill me a bumper—here, sir, bless the king!

*Dur.* 'Would I were out of his dominions!—By this light, she'll make me drunk too!

*Bis.* O pardon me, sir, you shall do me right—fill it higher.
—Now, sir, can you drink a health under your leg?

*Dur.* Rare philosophy that, 'faith!

*Bis.* Come, off with it to the bottom!—Now, how d'ye like me, sir?

*Dur.* O, mighty well, madam!

*Bis.* You see how a woman's fancy varies! sometimes, splenetic and heavy, then, gay and frolicsome.—And how d'ye like the humour?

*Dur.* Good madam, let me sit down to answer you, for I am heartily tired.

*Bis.* Fie upon't! a young man, and tired! up, for shame, and walk about!—Action becomes us—a little faster, sir—What d'ye think now of my Lady La Pale, and Lady Coquet, the duke's fair daughter? Ha! Are they not brisk lasses? Then there is black Mrs. Bellair, and brown Mrs. Bellface!

*Dur.* They are all strangers to me, madam.

*Bis.* But let me tell you, sir, that brown is not always despicable—O Lard, sir, if young Mrs. Bagatell had kept herself single till this time o'day, what a beauty there had been! And then, you know, the charming Mrs. Monkeylove, the fair gem of St. Germain's!

*Dur.* Upon my soul, I don't!

*Bis.* And then, you must have heard of the English beau, Spleenamore, how unlike a gentleman——

*Dur.* Hey!—not a syllable on't, as I hope to be saved, madam!

*Bis.* No! Why, then, play me a jig;—[*Music.*]—Come, sir.

*Dur.* By this light, I cannot! 'faith, madam, I have sprained my leg!

*Bis.* Then sit you down, sir;—and now tell me what's your business with me? What's your errand? Quick, quick, despatch!—Odso, may be, you are some gentleman's servant, that has brought me a letter, or a haunch of venison?

*Dur.* 'Sdeath, madam, do I look like a carrier?

*Bis.* O, cry you mercy, I saw you just now, I mistook you, upon my word! you are one of the travelling gentlemen—and pray, sir, how do all our impudent friends in Italy?

*Dur.* Madam, I came to wait on you with a more serious intention than your entertainment has answered.

*Bis.* Sir, your intention of waiting on me was the greatest affront imaginable, however your expressions may turn it to a compliment: Your visit, sir, was intended as a prologue to a very scurvy play, of which, Mr. Mirabel and you so handsomely laid the plot.—"Marry! No, no, I am a man of more honour."—Where's your honour? Where's your courage now? Ads my life, sir, I have a great mind to kick you!—Go, go to your fellow-rake now, rail at my sex, and get drunk for vexation, and write a lampoon—But I must have you to know, sir, that my reputation is above the scandal of a libel, my virtue is sufficiently approved to those whose opinion is my interest: and, for the rest, let them talk what they will; for, when I please, I'll be what I please, in spite of you and all mankind; and so, my dear man of honour, if you be tired, con over this lesson, and sit there till I come to you.[*Runs off.*

*Dur.* Tum ti dum. [*Sings.*] Ha! ha! ha! "Ad's my life, I have a great mind to kick you!"—Oons and confusion! [*Starts up.*] Was ever man so abused!—Ay, Mirabel set me on.

*Enter* PETIT.

*Petit.* Well, sir, how d'ye find yourself?

*Dur.* You son of a nine-eyed whore, d'ye come to abuse me? I'll kick you with a vengeance, you dog!

[PETIT *runs off, and* DURETETE *after him.*

25

# ACT THE THIRD.

## SCENE I.

OLD MIRABEL'S *House.*

*Enter* OLD *and* YOUNG MIRABEL, *meeting.*

*Old Mir.* Bob, come hither, Bob.

*Y. Mir.* Your pleasure, sir?

*Old Mir.* Are not you a great rogue, sirrah?

*Y. Mir.* That's a little out of my comprehension, sir; for I've heard say, that I resemble my father.

*Old Mir.* Your father is your very humble slave—I tell thee what, child, thou art a very pretty fellow, and I love thee heartily; and a very great villain, and I hate thee mortally.

*Y. Mir.* Villain, sir! Then I must be a very impudent one; for I can't recollect any passage of my life that I'm ashamed of.

*Old Mir.* Come hither, my dear friend; dost see this picture?

[*Shows him a little Picture.*

*Y. Mir.* Oriana's? Pshaw!

*Old Mir.* What, sir, won't you look upon't?—Bob, dear Bob, pr'ythee come hither now—Dost want any money, child?

*Y. Mir.* No, sir.

*Old Mir.* Why, then, here's some for thee: come here now— How canst thou be so hard-hearted, an unnatural, unmannerly rascal, (don't mistake me, child, I a'n't angry) as to abuse this tender, lovely, good-natured, dear rogue?—Why, she sighs for thee, and cries for thee, pouts for thee, and snubs for thee; the poor little heart of it is like to burst——Come, my dear boy, be good-natured, like your own father; be now—and then, see here, read this——the effigies of the lovely Oriana, with thirty thousand pound to her portion—thirty thousand pound, you dog! thirty thousand pound, you rogue! how dare you refuse a lady with thirty thousand pound, you impudent rascal?

*Y. Mir.* Will you hear me speak, sir?

*Old Mir.* Hear you speak, sir! If you had thirty thousand tongues, you could not out-talk thirty thousand pound, sir.

*Y. Mir.* Nay, sir, if you won't hear me, I'll begone, sir! I'll take post for Italy this moment.

*Old Mir.* Ah, the fellow knows I won't part with him! Well, sir, what have you to say?

*Y. Mir.* The universal reception, sir, that marriage has had in the world, is enough to fix it for a public good, and to draw every body into the common cause; but there are some constitutions, like some instruments, so peculiarly singular, that they make tolerable music by themselves, but never do well in a concert.

*Old Mir.* Why, this is reason, I must confess, but yet it is nonsense too; for, though you should reason like an angel, if you argue yourself out of a good estate, you talk like a fool.

*Y. Mir.* But, sir, if you bribe me into bondage with the riches of Crœsus, you leave me but a beggar, for want of my liberty.

*Old Mir.* Was ever such a perverse fool heard? 'Sdeath, sir! why did I give you education? was it to dispute me out of my senses? Of what colour, now, is the head of this cane? You'll say, 'tis white, and, ten to one, make me believe it too——I thought that young fellows studied to get money.

*Y. Mir.* No, sir, I have studied to despise it; my reading was not to make me rich, but happy, sir.

*Old Mir.* There he has me again, now! But, sir, did not I marry to oblige you?

*Y. Mir.* To oblige me, sir! in what respect, pray?

*Old Mir.* Why, to bring you into the world, sir; wa'n't that an obligation?

*Y. Mir.* And, because I would have it still an obligation, I avoid marriage.

*Old Mir.* How is that, sir?

*Y. Mir.* Because I would not curse the hour I was born.

*Old Mir.* Lookye, friend, you may persuade me out of my designs, but I'll command you out of yours; and, though you may convince my reason that you are in the right, yet there is an old attendant of sixty-three, called positiveness, which you, nor all the wits in Italy, shall ever be able to shake: so, sir, you're a wit, and I'm a father: you may talk, but I'll be obeyed.

*Y. Mir.* This it is to have the son a finer gentleman than the father; they first give us breeding, that they don't understand; then they turn us out of doors, because we are wiser than themselves. But I'm a little aforehand with the old gentleman. [*Aside.*] Sir, you have been pleased to settle a thousand pound sterling a year upon me; in return of which, I have a very great honour for you and your family, and shall take care that your only and beloved son shall do nothing to make him hate his father, or to hang himself. So, dear sir, I'm your very humble servant.[*Runs off.*

*Old Mir.* Here, sirrah! rogue! Bob! villain!

*Enter* DUGARD.

*Dug.* Ah, sir! 'tis but what he deserves.

*Old Mir.* 'Tis false, sir! he don't deserve it: what have you to say against my boy, sir?

*Dug.* I shall only repeat your own words.

*Old Mir.* What have you to do with my words? I have swallowed my words already; I have eaten them up.—I say, that Bob's an honest fellow, and who dares deny it?

*Enter* BISARRE.

*Bis.* That dare I, sir:—I say, that your son is a wild, foppish, whimsical, impertinent coxcomb; and, were I abused, as this gentleman's sister is, I would make it an Italian quarrel, and poison the whole family.

*Dug.* Come, sir, 'tis no time for trifling: my sister is abused; you are made sensible of the affront, and your honour is concerned to see her redressed.

*Old Mir.* Lookye, Mr. Dugard, good words go farthest. I will do your sister justice, but it must be after my own rate; nobody must abuse my son but myself; for, although Robin be a sad dog, yet he's nobody's puppy but my own.

*Bis.* Ay, that's my sweet-natured, kind, old gentleman—

29

[*Wheedling him.*] We will be good, then, if you'll join with us in the plot.

*Old Mir.* Ah, you coaxing young baggage! what plot can you have to wheedle a fellow of sixty-three?

*Bis.* A plot that sixty-three is only good for; to bring other people together, sir. You must act the Spaniard, because your son will least suspect you; and, if he should, your authority protects you from a quarrel, to which Oriana is unwilling to expose her brother.

*Old Mir.* And what part will you act in the business, madam?

*Bis.* Myself, sir; my friend is grown a perfect changeling: these foolish hearts of ours spoil our heads presently; the fellows no sooner turn knaves, but we turn fools: but I am still myself, and he may expect the most severe usage from me, because I neither love him, nor hate him.[*Exit.*

*Old Mir.* Well said, Mrs. Paradox! but, sir, who must open the matter to him?

*Dug.* Petit, sir; who is our engineer general; and here he comes.

*Enter* Petit.

*Petit.* O, sir, more discoveries! are all friends about us?

*Dug.* Ay, ay, speak freely.

*Petit.* You must know, sir,——od's my life, I'm out of breath! you must know, sir,—you must know—

*Old Mir.* What the devil must we know, sir?

*Petit.* That I have [*Pants and blows.*] bribed, sir, bribed—your son's secretary of state.

*Old Mir.* Secretary of state!—who's that, for Heaven's sake?

*Petit.* His valet de chambre, sir? You must know, sir, that the intrigue lay folded up in his master's clothes; and, when he went to dust the embroidered suit, the secret flew out of the right pocket of his coat, in a whole swarm of your crambo songs, short-footed odes, and long-legged pindarics.

*Old Mir.* Impossible!

*Petit.* Ah, sir, he has loved her all along; there was Oriana in every line, but he hates marriage. Now, sir, this plot will stir up his jealousy, and we shall know, by the strength of that, how to proceed farther.

> Come, sir, let's about it with speed:
> 'Tis expedition gives our king the sway;
> For expedition to the French give way;
> Swift to attack, or swift—to run away.

[*Exeunt.*

*Enter* YOUNG MIRABEL *and* BISARRE, *passing carelessly by one another.*

*Bis.* [*Aside.*] I wonder what she can see in this fellow, to like him?

*Y. Mir.* [*Aside.*] I wonder what my friend can see in this girl, to admire her?

*Bis.* [*Aside.*] A wild, foppish, extravagant, rake-hell!

*Y. Mir.* [*Aside.*] A light, whimsical, impertinent, madcap!

*Bis.* Whom do you mean, sir?

*Y. Mir.* Whom do you mean, madam?

*Bis.* A fellow, that has nothing left to re-establish him for a human creature, but a prudent resolution to hang himself!

*Y. Mir.* There is a way, madam, to force me to that resolution.

*Bis.* I'll do it, with all my heart.

*Y. Mir.* Then you must marry me.

*Bis.* Lookye, sir, don't think your ill manners to me, shall excuse your ill usage of my friend; nor, by fixing a quarrel here, to divert my zeal for the absent; for I'm resolved, nay, I come prepared, to make you a panegyric, that shall mortify your pride, like any modern dedication.

*Y. Mir.* And I, madam, like a true modern patron, shall hardly give you thanks for your trouble.

31

*Bis.* Come, sir, to let you see what little foundation you have for your dear sufficiency, I'll take you to pieces.

*Y. Mir.* And what piece will you chuse?

*Bis.* Your heart, to be sure; because I should get presently rid on't: your courage I would give to a Hector, your wit to a lewd playmaker, your honour to an attorney, your body to the physicians, and your soul to its master.

*Y. Mir.* I had the oddest dream last night of the Duchess of Burgundy; methought the furbelows of her gown were pinned up so high behind, that I could not see her head for her tail.

*Bis.* The creature don't mind me! do you think, sir, that your humorous impertinence can divert me? No, sir, I'm above any pleasure that you can give, but that of seeing you miserable. And mark me, sir, my friend, my injured friend, shall yet be doubly happy, and you shall be a husband, as much as the rites of marriage, and the breach of them, can make you.

> [*Here* MIRABEL *pulls out a Virgil, and reads*
> *to himself, while she speaks.*

*Mir.* [Reading.]

> *At Regina dolos, (quis fallere possit amantem?)*
> *Dissimulare etiam sperásti perfide tantum—*

Very true.

> *Posse nefas.*

By your favour, friend Virgil, 'twas but a rascally trick of your hero, to forsake poor pug so inhumanly.

*Bis.* I don't know what to say to him. The devil——what's Virgil to us, sir?

*Mir.* Very much, madam; the most apropos in the world—for, what should I chop upon, but the very place where the perjured rogue of a lover, and the forsaken lady, are battling it tooth and nail! Come, madam, spend your spirits no longer; we'll take an easier method: I'll be Æneas now, and you shall be Dido, and we'll rail by book. Now for you, Madam Dido:

*Nec te noster amor, nec te data dextera quondam,*
*Nec Meritura tenet crudeli funere Dido——*

Ah, poor Dido![*Looking at her.*

*Bis.* Rudeness! affronts! impatience! I could almost start out, even to manhood, and want but a weapon, as long as his, to fight him upon the spot. What shall I say?

*Mir.* Now she rants.

*Quæ quibus anteferam? jam jam nec Maxima Juno.*

*Bis.* A man! No, the woman's birth was spirited away.

*Mir.* Right, right, madam, the very words.

*Bis.* And some pernicious elf left in the cradle, with human shape, to palliate growing mischief.

[*Both speak together, and raise their Voices by Degrees.*

Mir. *Perfide, sed duris genuit te Cautibus horrens*
*Caucasus, Hyrcanæque admorunt Ubera Tigres.*

*Bis.* Go, sir, fly to your midnight revels——

*Mir.* Excellent!

*I sequere Italiam ventis, pete regna per undas,*
*Spero equidem mediis, si quid pia Numina possunt.*

[Together again.

*Bis.* Converse with imps of darkness of your make; your nature starts at justice, and shivers at the touch of virtue.— Now, the devil take his impudence! He vexes me so, I don't know whether to cry or laugh at him.

*Mir.* Bravely performed, my dear Libyan! I'll write the tragedy of Dido, and you shall act the part; but you do nothing at all, unless you fret yourself into a fit; for here the poor lady is stifled with vapours, drops into the arms of her maids, and the cruel, barbarous, deceitful, wanderer, is, in the very next line, called pious Æneas.—There's authority for ye.

Sorry indeed Æneas stood,
    To see her in a pout;
But Jove himself, who ne'er thought good
    To stay a second bout,
Commands him off, with all his crew,
And leaves poor Dy, as I leave you.

[*Runs off.*

*Bis.* Go thy ways, for a dear, mad, deceitful, agreeable fellow! O' my conscience, I must excuse Oriana.

That lover soon his angry fair disarms,
Whose slighting pleases, and whose faults are charms.[*Exit.*

    *Enter* PETIT; *runs about to every Door, and knocks.*

*Petit.* Mr. Mirabel! Sir, where are you? no where to be found?

            *Enter* YOUNG MIRABEL.

*Y. Mir.* What's the matter, Petit?

*Petit.* Most critically met!—Ah, sir, that one who has followed the game so long, and brought the poor hare just under his paws, should let a mungrel cur chop in, and run away with the puss!

*Y. Mir.* If your worship can get out of your allegories, be pleased to tell me, in three words, what you mean.

*Petit.* Plain, plain, sir! Your mistress and mine is going to be married!

*Y. Mir.* I believe you lie, sir.

*Petit.* Your humble servant, sir.[*Going.*

*Y. Mir.* Come hither, Petit. Married, say you?

*Petit.* No, sir, 'tis no matter: I only thought to do you a service; but I shall take care how I confer my favours for the future.

*Y. Mir.* Sir, I beg ten thousand pardons.[*Bowing low.*

*Petit.* 'Tis enough, sir.—I come to tell you, sir, that Oriana is this moment to be sacrificed; married past redemption!

*Y. Mir.* I understand her; she'll take a husband, out of spite to me, and then, out of love to me, she will make him a cuckold! But who is the happy man?

*Petit.* A lord, sir.

*Y. Mir.* I'm her ladyship's most humble servant. Now must I be a constant attender at my lord's levee, to work my way to my lady's couchee——A countess, I presume, sir——

*Petit.* A Spanish count, sir, that Mr. Dugard knew abroad, is come to Paris, saw your mistress yesterday, marries her to-day, and whips her into Spain to-morrow.

*Y. Mir.* Ay, is it so? and must I follow my cuckold over the Pyrenees? Had she married within the precincts of a billet-doux, I would be the man to lead her to church; but, as it happens, I'll forbid the banns! Where is this mighty don?

*Petit.* Have a care, sir; he's a rough cross-grained piece, and there's no tampering with him. Would you apply to Mr. Dugard, or the lady herself, something might be done, for it is in despite to you, that the business is carried so hastily. Odso, sir, here he comes! I must be gone.[*Exit.*

Enter OLD MIRABEL, *dressed in a Spanish Habit, leading* ORIANA.

*Oriana.* Good my lord, a nobler choice had better suited your lordship's merit. My person, rank, and circumstance, expose me as the public theme of raillery, and subject me so to injurious usage, my lord, that I can lay no claim to any part of your regard, except your pity.

*Old Mir.* Breathes he vital air, that dares presume,
With rude behaviour, to profane such excellence?
Show me the man——
And you shall see how my sudden revenge
Shall fall upon the head of such presumption.
Is this thing one?

[*Strutting up to* YOUNG MIRABEL.

*Y. Mir.* Sir!

*Oriana.* Good my lord.

*Old Mir.* If he, or any he!

*Oriana.* Pray, my lord, the gentleman's a stranger.

*Old Mir.* O, your pardon, sir,—but if you had—remember, sir,—the lady now is mine, her injuries are mine; therefore, sir, you understand me——Come, madam.

> [*Leads* ORIANA *to the Door; she goes off;*
> YOUNG MIRABEL *runs to his Father, and*
> *pulls him by the Sleeve.*

Y. Mir. *Ecoute, Monsieur le Count.*

*Old Mir.* Your business, sir?

*Y. Mir.* Boh!

*Old Mir.* Boh! what language is that, sir?

*Y. Mir.* Spanish, my lord.

*Old Mir.* What d'ye mean?

*Y. Mir.* This, sir.

> [*Trips up his Heels.*

*Old Mir.* A very concise quarrel, truly——I'll bully him. —*Trinidade Seigneur*, give me fair play.

> [*Offering to rise.*

*Y. Mir.* By all means, sir. [*Takes away his Sword.*] Now, seigneur, where's that bombast look, and fustian face, your countship wore just now?

> [*Strikes him.*

*Old Mir.* The rogue quarrels well, very well; my own son right!—But hold, sirrah, no more jesting; I'm your father, sir! your father!

*Y. Mir.* My father! Then, by this light, I could find in my heart to pay thee. [*Aside.*] Is the fellow mad? Why, sure, sir, I han't frighted you out of your senses?

*Old Mir.* But you have, sir!

*Y. Mir.* Then I'll beat them into you again.

*[Offers to strike him.*

*Old Mir.* Why, rogue!—Bob! dear Bob! don't you know me, child?

*Y. Mir.* Ha! ha! ha! the fellow's downright distracted! Thou miracle of impudence! wouldst thou make me believe, that such a grave gentleman as my father would go a masquerading thus? That a person of threescore and three would run about, in a fool's coat, to disgrace himself and family? why, you impudent villain, do you think I will suffer such an affront to pass upon my honoured father, my worthy father, my dear father? 'Sdeath, sir! mention my father but once again, and I'll send your soul to thy grandfather this minute!

*[Offering to stab him.*

*Old Mir.* Well, well, I am not your father.

*Y. Mir.* Why, then, sir, you are the saucy, hectoring Spaniard, and I'll use you accordingly.

*Enter* DUGARD, ORIANA, MAID, *and* PETIT. DUGARD *runs to* YOUNG MIRABEL, *the rest to the Old Gentleman.*

*Dug.* Fie, fie, Mirabel! murder your father!

*Y. Mir.* My father? What, is the whole family mad? Give me way, sir, I won't be held.

*Old Mir.* No? nor I neither; let me begone, pray.

*[Offering to go.*

*Y. Mir.* My father!

*Old Mir.* Ay, you dog's face! I am your father, for I have borne as much for thee, as your mother ever did.

*Y. Mir.* O ho! then this was a trick, it seems, a design, a contrivance, a stratagem!—Oh, how my bones ache!

*Old Mir.* Your bones, sirrah! why yours?

*Y. Mir.* Why sir, han't I been beating my own flesh and blood all this while? O, madam, [*To* ORIANA.] I wish your ladyship joy of your new dignity. Here was a contrivance

37

indeed!

*Oriana.* Pray, sir, don't insult the misfortunes of your own creating.

*Dug.* My prudence will be counted cowardice, if I stand tamely now.—[*Comes up between* Young Mirabel *and his Sister.*] Well, sir!

*Y. Mir.* Well, sir! Do you take me for one of your tenants, sir, that you put on your landlord's face at me?

*Dug.* On what presumption, sir, dare you assume thus? [*Draws.*

*Old Mir.* What's that to you, sir?[*Draws.*

*Petit.* Help! help! the lady faints!

[Oriana *falls into her Maid's Arms.*

*Y. Mir.* Vapours! vapours! she'll come to herself: If it be an angry fit, a dram of assa fœtida—If jealousy, hartshorn in water—if the mother, burnt feathers—If grief, ratafia—If it be straight stays, or corns, there's nothing like a dram of plain brandy.[*Exit.*

*Oriana.* Hold off, give me air——O, my brother! would you preserve my life, endanger not your own; would you defend my reputation, leave it to itself; 'tis a dear vindication that's purchased by the sword; for, though our champion proves victorious, yet our honour is wounded.

*Old Mir.* Ay, and your lover may be wounded, that's another thing. But I think you are pretty brisk again, my child.

*Oriana.* Ay, sir, my indisposition was only a pretence to divert the quarrel; the capricious taste of your sex, excuses this artifice in ours.[*Exit.*

*Petit.* Come, Mr. Dugard, take courage; there is a way still left to fetch him again.

*Old Mir.* Sir, I'll have no plot that has any relation to Spain.

*Dug.* I scorn all artifice whatsoever; my sword shall do her justice.

*Petit.* Pretty justice, truly! Suppose you run him through the body, you run her through the heart at the same time.

*Old Mir.* And me through the head—rot your sword, sir, we'll have plots! Come, Petit, let's hear.

*Petit.* What if she pretended to go into a nunnery, and so bring him about to declare himself?

*Dug.* That, I must confess, has a face.

*Old Mir.* A face! a face like an angel, sir! Ad's my life, sir, 'tis the most beautiful plot in Christendom! We'll about it immediately.[*Exeunt.*

---

# ACT THE FOURTH

## SCENE I.

Old Mirabel's *House.*

*Enter* Old Mirabel *and* Dugard.

*Dug.* The Lady Abbess is my relation, and privy to the plot.

*Old Mir.* Ay, ay, this nunnery will bring him about, I warrant ye.

*Enter* Duretete.

*Dur.* Here, where are ye all?—O, Mr. Mirabel! you have done fine things for your posterity—And you, Mr. Dugard, may come to answer this—I come to demand my friend at your hands; restore him, sir, or——

[*To* Old Mirabel.

*Old Mir.* Restore him! What, d'ye think I have got him in my trunk, or my pocket?

*Dur.* Sir, he's mad, and you are the cause on't.

*Old Mir.* That may be; for I was as mad as he when I begot him.

*Dug.* Mad, sir! What d'ye mean?

*Dur.* What do you mean, sir, by shutting up your sister, yonder, to talk like a parrot through a cage? or a decoy-duck, to draw others into the snare? Your son, sir, because she has deserted him, he has forsaken the world; and, in three words, has——

*Old Mir.* Hanged himself!

*Dur.* The very same—turned friar!

*Old Mir.* You lie, sir! 'tis ten times worse. Bob turned friar! —Why should the fellow shave his foolish crown, when the same razor may cut his throat?

*Dur.* If you have any command, or you any interest over him, lose not a minute: He has thrown himself into the next monastery, and has ordered me to pay off his servants, and discharge his equipage.

*Old Mir.* Let me alone to ferret him out: I'll sacrifice the Abbot, if he receives him; I'll try whether the spiritual or the natural father has the most right to the child.—But, dear Captain, what has he done with his estate?

*Dur.* Settled it upon the church, sir.

*Old Mir.* The church! Nay, then the devil won't get him out of their clutches——Ten thousand livres a year upon the church!—'Tis downright sacrilege—Come, gentlemen, all hands to work: for half that sum, one of these monasteries shall protect you a traitor from the law, a rebellious wife from her husband, and a disobedient son from his own father.[*Exit.*

*Dug.* But will ye persuade me that he's gone to a monastery?

*Dur.* Is your sister gone to the Filles Repenties? I tell you, sir, she's not fit for the society of repenting maids.

*Dug.* Why so, sir?

*Dur.* Because she's neither one nor t'other; she's too old to be a maid, and too young to repent.

*[Exit*—DUGARD *after him.*

## SCENE II.

*The Inside of a Monastery.*

*Enter* ORIANA, *in a Nun's Habit, and* BISARRE.

*Oriana.* I hope, Bisarre, there is no harm in jesting with this religious habit.

*Bis.* To me, the greatest jest in the habit, is taking it in earnest.

*Oriana.* But I'm reconciled, methinks, to the mortification of a nunnery; because I fancy the habit becomes me.

*Bis.* A well-contrived mortification, truly, that makes a woman look ten times handsomer than she did before!—Ay, my dear, were there any religion in becoming dress, our sex's devotion were rightly placed; for our toilets would do the work of the altar; we should all be canonized.

*Oriana.* But don't you think there is a great deal of merit in dedicating a beautiful face and person to the service of religion?

*Bis.* Not half so much as devoting them to a pretty fellow. Come, come, mind your business. Mirabel loves you, 'tis now plain, and hold him to't; give fresh orders that he shan't see you: we get more by hiding our faces, sometimes, than by exposing them; a very mask, you see, whets desire; but a pair of keen eyes, through an iron grate, fire double upon them, with view and disguise. But I must begone upon my affairs; I have brought my captain about again.

*Oriana.* But why will you trouble yourself with that coxcomb?

*Bis.* Because he is a coxcomb: had I not better have a lover like him, that I can make an ass of, than a lover like yours, to make a fool of me. [*Knocking below.*] A message from

41

Mirabel, I'll lay my life! [*She runs to the Door.*] Come hither! run, thou charming nun, come hither!

*Oriana.* What's the news?[*Runs to her.*

*Bis.* Don't you see who's below?

*Oriana.* I see nobody but a friar.

*Bis.* Ah, thou poor blind Cupid! A friar! Don't you see a villanous genteel mien, under that cloak of hypocrisy?

*Oriana.* As I live, Mirabel turned friar! I hope, in Heaven, he's not in earnest.

*Bis.* In earnest! Ha! ha! ha! are you in earnest? Remember what I say, if you would yield to advantage, and hold out the attack; to draw him on, keep him off, to be sure.

> The cunning gamesters never gain too fast,
> But lose at first, to win the more at last.

[*Exit.*

*Enter* YOUNG MIRABEL, *in a Friar's Habit.*

*Y. Mir.* 'Save you, sister—Your brother, young lady, having a regard for your soul's health, has sent me to prepare you for the sacred habit, by confession.

*Oriana.* My brother's care I own; and to you, sacred sir, I confess, that the great crying sin, which I have long indulged, and now prepare to expiate, was love. My morning thoughts, my evening prayers, my daily musings, nightly cares, was love!

*Y. Mir.* She's downright stark mad in earnest! Death and confusion, I have lost her! [*Aside.*]—You confess your fault, madam, in such moving terms, that I could almost be in love with the sin.

*Oriana.* Take care, sir; crimes, like virtues, are their own rewards; my chief delight became my only grief; he, in whose breast I thought my heart secure, turned robber, and despoiled the treasure that he kept.

*Y. Mir.* Perhaps that treasure he esteemed so much, that, like the miser, though afraid to use it, he reserves it safe.

42

*Oriana.* No, holy father: who can be miser in another's wealth, that's prodigal of his own? His heart was open, shared to all he knew, and what, alas! must then become of mine! But the same eyes, that drew this passion in, shall send it out in tears, to which now hear my vow——

*Y. Mir.* [*Discovering himself.*] No, my fair angel! Here, on my knees, behold the criminal, that vows repentance his. [*Kneels.*] Ha! no concern upon her!

Enter OLD MIRABEL.

*Old Mir.* Where, where's this counterfeit nun?

*Oriana.* Madness! confusion! I'm ruined!

*Y. Mir.* What do I hear? [*Puts on his Hood.*] What did you say, sir?

*Old Mir.* I say she's a counterfeit, and you may be another, for aught I know, sir: I have lost my child by these tricks, sir.

*Y. Mir.* What tricks, sir?

*Old Mir.* By a pretended trick, sir. A contrivance to bring my son to reason, and it has made him stark mad; I have lost him, and a thousand pound a year.

*Y. Mir.* [*Discovering himself.*] My dear father, I'm your most humble servant.

*Old Mir.* My dear boy! [*Runs and kisses him.*]—Welcome, *ex inferis,* my dear boy! 'tis all a trick, she's no more a nun than I am.

*Y. Mir.* No!

*Old Mir.* The devil a bit.

*Y. Mir.* Then kiss me again, my dear dad, for the most happy news—And now, most venerable holy sister,[*Kneels.*

> Your mercy and your pardon I implore,
> For the offence of asking it before.

Lookye, my dear counterfeiting nun, take my advice, be a nun in good earnest; women make the best nuns always, when they can't do otherwise.

*Oriana.* O, sir! how unhappily have you destroyed what was so near perfection! He is the counterfeit, that has deceived you.

*Old Mir.* Ha! Lookye, sir, I recant; she is a nun.

*Y. Mir.* Sir, your humble servant; then I'm a friar this moment.

*Old Mir.* Was ever an old fool so bantered by a brace o' young ones! Hang you both! you're both counterfeits, and my plot's spoiled, that's all.

*Oriana.* Shame and confusion, love, anger, and disappointment, will work my brain to madness!

[*Takes off her Habit—Exit.*

*Y. Mir.* Ay, ay, throw by the rags; they have served a turn for us both, and they shall e'en go off together.

[*Takes off his Habit.*
[*Exit, throwing away the Habit.*

## SCENE III.

OLD MIRABEL'S *House.*

*Enter* DURETETE, *with a Letter.*

*Dur.* [Reads.] *My rudeness was only a proof of your humour, which I have found so agreeable, that I own myself penitent, and willing to make any reparation upon your first appearance to*BISARRE.

Mirabel swears she loves me, and this confirms it; then farewell gallantry, and welcome revenge! 'Tis my turn now to be upon the sublime; I'll take her off; I warrant her!

*Enter* BISARRE.

Well, mistress, do you love me?

*Bis.* I hope, sir, you will pardon the modesty of——

44

*Dur.* Of what? of a dancing devil!—Do you love me, I say?

*Bis.* Perhaps I——

*Dur.* What?

*Bis.* Perhaps I do not.

*Dur.* Ha! abused again! Death, woman, I'll——

*Bis.* Hold, hold, sir! I do, do!

*Dur.* Confirm it, then, by your obedience; stand there, and ogle me now, as if your heart, blood, and soul, were like to fly out at your eyes—First, the direct surprise. [*She looks full upon him.*] Right; next, the *deux yeux par oblique.* [*She gives him the side Glance.*] Right; now depart, and languish. [*She turns from him, and looks over her Shoulder.*] Very well; now sigh. [*She sighs.*] Now drop your fan on purpose. [*She drops her Fan.*] Now take it up again. Come now, confess your faults; are not you a proud—say after me.

*Bis.* Proud.

*Dur.* Impertinent.

*Bis.* Impertinent.

*Dur.* Ridiculous.

*Bis.* Ridiculous.

*Dur.* Flirt.

*Bis.* Puppy.

*Dur.* Zoons! Woman, don't provoke me; we are alone, and you don't know but the devil may tempt me to do you a mischief; ask my pardon immediately.

*Bis.* I do, sir; I only mistook the word.

*Dur.* Cry, then. Have you got e'er a handkerchief?

*Bis.* Yes, sir.

*Dur.* Cry, then, handsomely; cry like a queen in a tragedy.

> [*She pretending to cry, bursts out a laughing.*
>
> *Enter Two* LADIES, *laughing.*

*Bis.* Ha! ha! ha!

*Both Ladies.* Ha! ha! ha!

*Dur.* Hell broke loose upon me, and all the furies fluttered about my ears! Betrayed again?

*Bis.* That you are, upon my word, my dear Captain; ha! ha! ha!

*Dur.* The Lord deliver me!

*1 Lady.* What! is this the mighty man, with the bull-face, that comes to frighten ladies?

*Dur.* Ah, madam, I'm the best natured fellow in the world.

*Bis.* A man! we're mistaken; a man has manners: the awkward creature is some tinker's trull, in a periwig. Come, ladies, let us examine him.

> [*They lay hold on him.*

*Dur.* Examine! the devil you will!

*Bis.* I'll lay my life, some great dairy maid in man's clothes!

*Dur.* They will do't;—lookye, dear christian women! pray hear me.

*Bis.* Will you ever attempt a lady's honour again?

*Dur.* If you please to let me get away with my honour, I'll do any thing in the world.

*Bis.* Will you persuade your friend to marry mine?

*Dur.* O yes, to be sure.

*Bis.* And will you do the same by me?

*Dur.* Burn me if I do, if the coast be clear.[*Runs out.*

*Bis.* Ha! ha! ha! The visit, ladies, was critical for our diversions: we'll go make an end of our tea.[*Exeunt.*

> *Enter* YOUNG MIRABEL *and* OLD MIRABEL.

*Y. Mir.* Your patience, sir. I tell you, I won't marry; and, though you send all the bishops in France to persuade me, I shall never believe their doctrine against their practice. You would compel me to that state, which I have heard you curse yourself, when my mother and you have battled it for a whole week together.

*Old Mir.* Never but once, you rogue, and that was when she longed for six Flanders mares: ay, sir, then she was breeding of you, which showed what an expensive dog I should have of you.

*Enter* PETIT.

Well, Petit, how does she now?

*Petit.* Mad, sir, *con pompos*—Ay, Mr. Mirabel, you'll believe that I speak truth, now, when I confess that I have told you hitherto nothing but lies: our jesting is come to a sad earnest; she's downright distracted!

*Enter* BISARRE.

*Bis.* Where is this mighty victor!——The great exploit is done. O, sir, [*To the old Gentleman.*] your wretched ward has found a tender guardian of you, where her young innocence expected protection, here has she found her ruin.

*Old Mir.* Ay, the fault is mine; for I believe that rogue won't marry, for fear of begetting such another disobedient son as his father did. I have done all I can, madam, and now can do no more than run mad for company.[*Cries.*

*Enter* DUGARD, *with his Sword drawn.*

*Dug.* Away! Revenge! Revenge!

*Old Mir.* Patience! Patience, sir! [OLD MIRABEL *holds him.*] Bob, draw.[*Aside.*

*Dug.* Patience! the coward's virtue, and the brave man's failing, when thus provoked—Villain!

*Y. Mir.* Your sister's phrensy shall excuse your madness; and, to show my concern for what she suffers, I'll bear the villain from her brother.—Put up your anger with your sword; I have a heart like yours, that swells at an affront received, but melts at an injury given; and, if the lovely Oriana's grief be such a moving scene, 'twill find a part within this breast, perhaps as tender as a brother's.

*Dug.* To prove that soft compassion for her grief, endeavour to remove it.—There, there, behold an object that's infective; I cannot view her, but I am as mad as she!

*Enter* ORIANA, *held by Two Maids, who put her in a Chair.*

A sister, that my dying parents left, with their last words and blessing, to my care. Sister, dearest sister![*Goes to her.*

*Old Mir.* Ay, poor child, poor child, d'ye know me?

*Oriana.* You! you are Amadis de Gaul, sir.—Oh! oh, my heart! Were you never in love, fair lady? And do you never dream of flowers and gardens?—I dream of walking fires, and tall gigantic sights. Take heed, it comes now—What's that? Pray stand away: I have seen that face, sure.—How light my head is!

*Y. Mir.* What piercing charms has beauty, even in madness!

ORIANA:—I CANNOT; FOR I MUST BE UP AND GO
TO CHURCH

**Click to ENLARGE**

*Oriana.* I cannot; for I must be up to go to church, and I must dress me, put on my new gown, and be so fine, to meet my love. Heigho!—Will not you tell me where my heart lies buried?

*Y. Mir.* My very soul is touch'd—Your hand, my fair!

*Oriana.* How soft and gentle you feel! I'll tell you your fortune, friend.

*Y. Mir.* How she stares upon me!

*Oriana.* You have a flattering face; but 'tis a fine one—I warrant you have five hundred mistresses—Ay, to be sure, a mistress for every guinea in his pocket—Will you pray for me? I shall die to-morrow——And will you ring my passing bell?

*Y. Mir.* Do you know me, injured creature?

*Oriana.* No,—but you shall be my intimate acquaintance—in the grave.[*Weeps.*

*Y. Mir.* Oh, tears! I must believe you; sure there's a kind of sympathy in madness; for even I, obdurate as I am, do feel my soul so tossed with storms of passion, that I could cry for help as well as she.

[*Wipes his Eyes.*

*Oriana.* What, have you lost your lover? No, you mock me; I'll go home and pray.

*Y. Mir.* Stay, my fair innocence, and hear me own my love so loud, that I may call your senses to their place, restore them to their charming happy functions, and reinstate myself into your favour.

*Bis.* Let her alone, sir; 'tis all too late: she trembles; hold her, her fits grow stronger by her talking; don't trouble her, she don't know you, sir.

*Old Mir.* Not know him! what then? she loves to see him for all that.

*Enter* DURETETE.

*Dur.* Where are you all? What the devil! melancholy, and I

here! Are ye sad, and such a ridiculous subject, such a very good jest among you as I am?

*Y. Mir.* Away with this impertinence; this is no place for bagatelle; I have murdered my honour, destroyed a lady, and my desire of reparation is come at length too late. See there!

*Dur.* What ails her?

*Y. Mir.* Alas, she's mad!

*Dur.* Mad! dost wonder at that? By this light, they're all so; they're cozening mad; they're brawling mad; they're proud mad: I just now came from a whole world of mad women, that had almost—What, is she dead?

*Y. Mir.* Dead! Heavens forbid.

*Dur.* Heavens further it; for, till they be as cold as a key, there's no trusting them; you're never sure that a woman's in earnest, till she is nailed in her coffin. Shall I talk to her? Are you mad, mistress?

*Bis.* What's that to you, sir?

*Dur.* Oons, madam, are you there?[*Runs off.*

*Y. Mir.* Away, thou wild buffoon! How poor and mean this humour now appears? His follies and my own I here disclaim; this lady's phrensy has restored my senses, and, was she perfect now, as once she was, (before you all I speak it) she should be mine; and, as she is, my tears and prayers shall wed her.

*Dug.* How happy had this declaration been some hours ago!

*Bis.* Sir, she beckons to you, and waves us to go off: come, come, let's leave them.

[*Exeunt all but* YOUNG MIRABEL *and* ORIANA.

*Oriana.* Oh, sir!

*Y. Mir.* Speak, my charming angel, if your dear senses have regained their order; speak, fair, and bless me with the news.

*Oriana.* First, let me bless the cunning of my sex, that happy counterfeited phrensy that has restored to my poor labouring breast the dearest, best beloved of men.

*Y. Mir.* Tune all, ye spheres, your instruments of joy, and carry round your spacious orbs the happy sound of Oriana's health; her soul, whose harmony was next to yours, is now in tune again; the counterfeiting fair has played the fool!

> She was so mad, to counterfeit for me;
> I was so mad, to pawn my liberty:
> But now we both are well, and both are free.

*Oriana.* How, sir? Free!

*Y. Mir.* As air, my dear bedlamite! What, marry a lunatic! Lookye, my dear, you have counterfeited madness so very well this bout, that you'll be apt to play the fool all your life long.——Here, gentlemen!

*Oriana.* Monster! you won't disgrace me!

*Y. Mir.* O' my faith, but I will. Here, come in gentlemen.—A miracle! a miracle! the woman's dispossess'd! the devil's vanished!

*Enter* OLD MIRABEL *and* DUGARD.

*Old Mir.* Bless us! was she possessed?

*Y. Mir.* With the worst of demons, sir! a marriage devil! a horrid devil! Mr. Dugard, don't be surprised. I promised my endeavours to cure your sister; no mad doctor in Christendom could have done it more effectually. Take her into your charge; and have a care she don't relapse. If she should, employ me not again, for I am no more infallible than others of the faculty; I do cure sometimes.

*Oriana.* Your remedy, most barbarous man, will prove the greatest poison to my health; for, though my former phrensy was but counterfeit, I now shall run into a real madness.

[*Exit*; OLD MIRABEL *after.*

*Y. Mir.* What a dangerous precipice have I 'scap'd! Was not I just now upon the brink of destruction?

*Enter* DURETETE.

Oh, my friend, let me run into thy bosom! no lark escaped from the devouring pounces of a hawk, quakes with more dismal apprehension.

*Dur.* The matter, man!

*Y. Mir.* Marriage! hanging! I was just at the gallows foot, the running noose about my neck, and the cart wheeling from me. —Oh, I shan't be myself this month again!

*Dur.* Did not I tell you so? They are all alike, saints or devils!

*Y. Mir.* Ay, ay: there's no living here with security; this house is so full of stratagem and design, that I must abroad again.

*Dur.* With all my heart; I'll bear thee company, my lad: I'll meet you at the play; and we'll set out for Italy to-morrow morning.

*Y. Mir.* A match; I'll go pay my compliment of leave to my father presently.

*Dur.* I'm afraid he'll stop you.

*Y. Mir.* What, pretend a command over me, after his settlement of a thousand pound a year upon me! No, no, he has passed away his authority with the conveyance; the will of the living father is chiefly obeyed for the sake of the dying one.

> Dependence, ev'n a father's sway secures,
> For, though the son rebels, the heir is yours.

*[Exeunt severally.*

---

# ACT THE FIFTH.

## SCENE I.

*The Street before the Playhouse.*

MIRABEL *and* DURETETE, *as coming from the Play.*

*Dur.* How d'ye like this play?

*Y. Mir.* I liked the company;—the lady, the rich beauty, in the front box, had my attention: These impudent poets bring the ladies together to support them, and to kill every body else.

> *For deaths upon the stage, the ladies cry,*
> *But ne'er mind us, that in the audience die:*
> *The poet's hero should not move their pain,*
> *But they should weep for those their eyes have slain.*

*Dur.* Hoyty, toyty! did Phillis inspire you with all this?

*Y. Mir.* Ten times more; the playhouse is the element of poetry, because the region of beauty; the ladies, methinks, have a more inspiring, triumphant air in the boxes than any where else—they sit, commanding on their thrones, with all their subject slaves about them;—Their best clothes, best looks, shining jewels, sparkling eyes; the treasure of the world in a ring.—I could wish that my whole life long, were the first night of a new play.

*Dur.* The fellow has quite forgot this journey;—have you bespoke post horses?

*Y. Mir.* Grant me but three days, dear Captain, one to discover the lady, one to unfold myself, and one to make me happy, and then I'm yours to the world's end.

*Dur.* Hast thou the impudence to promise thyself a lady of her figure and quality in so short a time?

*Y. Mir.* Yes, sir; I have a confident address, no disagreeable person, and five hundred Lewis d'ors in my pocket.

*Dur.* Five hundred Lewis d'ors! you an't mad!

*Y. Mir.* I tell you, she's worth five thousand; one of her black, brilliant eyes, is worth a diamond as big as her head.

54

*Dur.* But you have owned to me, that, abating Oriana's pretensions to marriage, you loved her passionately; then how can you wander at this rate?

*Y. Mir.* I longed for a partridge t'other day, off the king's plate, but d'ye think, because I could not have it, I must eat nothing?

*Enter* ORIANA, *in Boy's Clothes, with a Letter.*

*Oriana.* Is your name Mirabel, sir?

*Y. Mir.* Yes, sir.

*Oriana.* A letter from your uncle, in Picardy.

[*Gives the Letter.*

*Y. Mir.* [*Reads.*]

*The bearer is the son of a protestant gentleman, who, flying for his religion, left me the charge of this youth.*—A pretty Boy!—*He's fond of some handsome service, that may afford him opportunity of improvement: your care of him will oblige,Yours.*

Hast a mind to travel, child?

*Oriana.* 'Tis my desire, sir; I should be pleased to serve a traveller in any capacity.

*Y. Mir.* A hopeful inclination; you shall along with me into Italy, as my page.

*Dur.* [*Noise without.*] Too handsome—The play's done, and some of the ladies come this way.

[LAMORCE *without, with her Train borne up by a* PAGE.

*Y. Mir.* Duretete, the very dear, identical she!

*Dur.* And what then?

*Y. Mir.* Why, 'tis she!

*Dur.* And what then, sir?

*Y. Mir.* Then!—Why, lookye, sirrah, the first piece of service I put upon you, is to follow that lady's coach, and bring me word where she lives. [*To* ORIANA.

*Oriana.* I don't know the town, sir, and am afraid of losing myself.

*Y. Mir.* Pshaw!

*Enter* LAMORCE *and* PAGE.

*Lam.* Page, what's become of all my people?

*Page.* I can't tell, madam; I can see no sign of your ladyship's coach.

*Lam.* That fellow has got into his old pranks, and fallen drunk somewhere;—none of the footmen there?

*Page.* Not one, madam.

*Lam.* These servants are the plague of our lives—what shall I do?

*Y. Mir.* By all my hopes, Fortune pimps for me! now, Duretete, for a piece of gallantry!

*Dur.* Why, you won't, sure?

*Y. Mir.* Won't, brute!—Let not your servants' neglect, madam, put your ladyship to any inconvenience; for you can't be disappointed of an equipage, whilst mine waits below: and, would you honour the master so far, he would be proud to pay his attendance.

*Dur.* Ay, to be sure! [*Aside.*

*Lam.* Sir, I won't presume to be troublesome, for my habitation is a great way off.

*Dur.* Very true, madam, and he's a little engaged; besides, madam—a hackney coach will do as well, madam.

*Y. Mir.* Rude beast, be quiet! [*To* DURETETE.] The farther from home, madam, the more occasion you have for a guard —pray, madam—

*Lam.* Lard, sir——

[*He seems to press, she to decline it, in dumb show.*

*Dur.* Ah! The devil's in his impudence! now he wheedles, she smiles—he flatters, she simpers—he swears, she believes —he's a rogue, and she's a w—— in a moment.

*Y. Mir.* Without there! my coach! Duretete, wish me joy!

[*Hands the Lady out.*

*Dur.* Wish you a——! Here, you little Picard, go follow your master, and he'll lead you——

*Oriana.* Whither, sir?

*Dur.* To the Academy, child—'tis the fashion with men of quality, to teach their pages their exercises—go.

*Oriana.* Won't you go with him too, sir? That woman may do him some harm, I don't like her.

*Dur.* Why, how now, Mr. Page, do you start up, to give laws of a sudden? Do you pretend to rise at court, and disapprove the pleasure of your betters?—Lookye, sirrah, if ever you would rise by a great man, be sure to be with him in his little actions; and, as a step to your advancement, follow your master immediately, and make it your hope, that he goes to a bagnio.

*Oriana.* Heavens forbid![*Exit.*

*Dur.* Now would I sooner take a cart in company of the hangman, than a coach with that woman:—What a strange antipathy have I taken against these creatures! a woman to me, is aversion upon aversion! a cheese, a cat, a breast of mutton, the squalling of children, the grinding of knives, and the snuff of a candle.


## SCENE II.

LAMORCE'S *Lodgings.*

*Enter* MIRABEL *and* LAMORCE.


*Lam.* To convince me, sir, that your service was something more than good breeding, please to lay out an hour of your company upon my desire, as you have already upon my necessity.

*Y. Mir.* Your desire, madam, has only prevented my request:
—My hours! Make them yours, madam, eleven, twelve, one,
two, three, and all that belong to those happy minutes.

*Lam.* But I must trouble you, sir, to dismiss your retinue,
because an equipage at my door, at this time of night, will not
be consistent with my reputation.

*Y. Mir.* By all means, madam, all but one little boy—Here,
page!

Enter ORIANA.

Order my coach and servants home, and do you stay; 'tis a
foolish country-boy, that knows nothing but innocence.

*Lam.* Innocence, sir! I should be sorry if you made any
sinister constructions of my freedom.

*Y. Mir.* O, madam, I must not pretend to remark upon any
body's freedom, having so entirely forfeited my own.

*Lam.* Well, sir, 'twere convenient towards our easy
correspondence, that we entered into a free confidence of each
other, by a mutual declaration of what we are, and what we
think of one another.—Now, sir, what are you?

*Y. Mir.* In three words, madam,—I am a gentleman, and have
five hundred pounds in my pocket.

*Lam.* And your name is——

*Y. Mir.* Mustapha.—Now, madam, the inventory of your
fortunes?

*Lam.* My name is Lamorce—my birth, noble; I was married
young, to a proud, rude, sullen, impetuous fellow;—the
husband spoiled the gentleman;—crying ruined my face, till at
last, I took heart, leaped out of a window, got away to my
friends, sued my tyrant, and recovered my fortune.—I lived
from fifteen to twenty, to please a husband; from twenty to
forty, I'm resolved to please myself, and from thence,
upwards, I'll humour the world.

*Y. Mir.* Ha! ha! ha! I rejoice in your good fortune, with all
my heart!

*Lam.* O, now I think on't, Mr. Mustapha, you have got the

finest ring there, I could scarcely believe it right; pray let me see it.

*Y. Mir.* Hum! Yes, madam, 'tis—'tis right—but—but—but—but—but it was given me by my mother—an old family ring, madam—an old-fashioned, family ring.

*Lam.* Ay, sir!—If you can entertain yourself for a moment, I'll wait on you immediately.

*Y. Mir.* Certainly the stars have been in a strange, intriguing humour, when I was born.—Ay, this night should I have had a bride in my arms, and that I should like well enough! But what should I have to-morrow night? The same. And what next night? The same. And what next night? The very same: Soup for breakfast, soup for dinner, soup for supper, and soup for breakfast again—But here's variety.

> *I love the fair, who freely gives her heart,*
> *That's mine by ties of nature, not of art;*
> *Who boldly owns whate'er her thoughts indite,*
> *And is too modest for a hypocrite.*

> [LAMORCE *appears at the Door; as he runs towards*
> *her, Four* BRAVOES *step in before her. He*
> *starts back.*

She comes, she comes—Hum, hum—Bitch—Murdered, murdered, to be sure! The cursed strumpet! To make me send away my servants—Nobody near me! These cut-throats always make sure work.——What shall I do? I have but one way. Are these gentlemen your relations, madam?

*Lam.* Yes, sir.

*Y. Mir.* Gentlemen, your most humble servant;—sir, your most faithful; yours, sir, with all my heart; your most obedient—come, gentlemen, [*Salutes all round.*] please to sit—no ceremony—next the lady, pray, sir.

*Lam.* Well, sir, and how d'ye like my friends? [*They all sit.*

*Y. Mir.* O, madam, the most finished gentlemen! I was never more happy in good company in my life; I suppose, sir, you have travelled?

*1 Bra.* Yes, sir.

*Y. Mir.* Which way, may I presume?

*1 Bra.* In a western barge, sir.

*Y. Mir.* Ha! ha! ha! very pretty! facetious pretty gentleman!

*Lam.* Ha! ha! ha! sir, you have got the prettiest ring upon your finger there—

*Y. Mir.* Ah! Madam, 'tis at your service, with all my heart!

*[Offering the Ring.*

*Lam.* By no means, sir, a family ring! [*Takes it.*

*Y. Mir.* No matter, madam.——Seven hundred pound, by this light![*Aside.*

*2 Bra.* Pray, sir, what's o'clock?

*Y. Mir.* Hum! Sir, I have left my watch at home.

*2 Bra.* I thought I saw the string of it, just now.

*Y. Mir.* Ods my life, sir, I beg your pardon, here it is!—but it don't go.

*[Putting it up.*

*Lam.* O dear sir, an English watch! Tompion's, I presume?

*Y. Mir.* D'ye like, it, madam? No ceremony—'tis at your service, with all my heart and soul!—Tompion's! Hang ye! [*Aside.*

*1 Bra.* But, sir, above all things, I admire the fashion and make, of your sword hilt!

*Y. Mir.* I'm mighty glad you like it, sir!

*1 Bra.* Will you part with it, sir?

*Y. Mir.* Sir, I won't sell it.

*1 Bra.* Not sell it, sir!

*Y. Mir.* No, gentlemen, but I'll bestow it, with all my heart! [*Offering it.*

*1 Bra.* O sir, we shall rob you!

*Y. Mir.* That you do, I'll be sworn! [*Aside.*] I have another at home; pray, sir,—Gentlemen, you're too modest—have I any thing else that you fancy?—Sir, will you do me a favour? [*To the First* Bravo.] I am extremely in love with that hat which you wear, will you do me the favour to change with me?

*1 Bra.* Lookye, sir, this is a family hat, and I would not part with it, but if you like it——[*They change Hats.*]—I want but a handsome pretence to quarrel with him—Some wine! Sir, your good health.

[*Pulls* Mirabel *by the Nose.*

*Y. Mir.* Oh, sir, your most humble servant! a pleasant frolic enough, to drink a man's health, and pull him by the nose! ha! ha! ha! the pleasantest, pretty-humoured gentleman——

*Lam.* Help the gentleman to a glass.

[Mirabel *drinks.*

*1 Bra.* How d'ye like the wine, sir?

*Y. Mir.* Very good o'the kind, sir:—But I tell ye what, I find we're all inclined to be frolicsome, and 'egad, for my own part, I was never more disposed to be merry; let's make a night on't, ha!—This wine is pretty, but I have such burgundy at home! Lookye, gentlemen, let me send for half a dozen flasks of my burgundy, I defy France to match it;—'twill make us all life, all air, pray, gentlemen.

*2 Bra.* Eh? Shall us have his burgundy?

*1 Bra.* Yes, 'faith, we'll have all we can; here, call up the gentleman's servant.—[*Exit* Footman.] What think you, Lamorce?

*Lam.* Yes, yes—Your servant is a foolish country boy, sir, he understands nothing but innocence.

*Y. Mir.* Ay, ay, madam.—Here, Page,——

*Enter* Oriana.

Take this key, and go to my butler, order him to send half a dozen flasks of the red burgundy, marked a thousand; and be sure you make haste, I long to entertain my friends here; my very good friends.

*Omnes.* Ah, dear sir!

*1 Bra.* Here, child, take a glass of wine—Your master and I have changed hats, honey, in a frolic.—Where had you this pretty boy, honest Mustapha?

*Oriana.* Mustapha!

*Y. Mir.* Out of Picardy—this is the first errand he has made for me, and if he does it right, I will encourage him.

*Oriana.* The red burgundy, sir?

*Y. Mir.* The red, marked a thousand, and be sure you make haste.

*Oriana.* I shall, sir.[*Exit.*

*1 Bra.* Sir, you were pleased to like my hat, have you any fancy for my coat?—Lookye, sir, it has served a great many honest gentlemen, very faithfully.

*Y. Mir.* The insolence of these dogs is beyond their cruelty! [*Aside.*

*Lam.* You're melancholy, sir.

*Y. Mir.* Only concerned, madam, that I should have no servant here but this little boy—he'll make some confounded blunder, I'll lay my life on't; I would not be disappointed of my wine, for the universe.

*Lam.* He'll do well enough, sir; but supper's ready; will you please to eat a bit, sir?

*Y. Mir.* O, madam, I never had a better stomach in my life.

*Lam.* Come, then, we have nothing but a plate of soup.

*Y. Mir.* Ah! the marriage soup I could dispense with now.

[*Aside.—Exit, handing the Lady.*

*2 Bra.* Shall we dispatch him?

*3 Bra.* To be sure; I think he knows me.

*1 Bra.* Ay, ay, dead men tell no tales; I han't the confidence to look a man in the face, after I have done him an injury, therefore we'll murder him.[*Exeunt.*

## SCENE III.

OLD MIRABEL'S *House.*

*Enter* DURETETE.

*Dur.* My friend has forsaken me, I have abandoned my mistress, my time lies heavy upon my hands, and my money burns in my pocket—But now I think on't, my myrmidons are upon duty to-night; I'll fairly stroll down to the guard, and nod away the night with my honest lieutenant, over a flask of wine, a story, and a pipe of tobacco.

[*Going off,* BISARRE *meets him.*

*Bis.* Who comes there? stand!

*Dur.* Heyday, now she's turned dragoon!

*Bis.* Lookye, sir, I'm told you intend to travel again.—I design to wait on you as far as Italy.

*Dur.* Then I'll travel into Wales.

*Bis.* Wales! What country's that?

*Dur.* The land of mountains, child; where you're never out of the way, 'cause there's no such thing as a highroad.

*Bis.* Rather, always in a high road, because you travel all upon hills; but be't as it will, I'll jog along with you.

*Dur.* But we intend to sail to the East Indies.

*Bis.* East, or West, 'tis all one to me; I'm tight and light, and the fitter for sailing.

*Dur.* But suppose we take through Germany, and drink hard?

*Bis.* Suppose I take through Germany and drink harder than you?

*Dur.* Suppose I go to a bawdy house?

*Bis.* Suppose I show you the way?

*Dur.* 'Sdeath, woman! will you go to the guard with me, and smoke a pipe?

*Bis.* Allons donc!

*Dur.* The devil's in the woman!—Suppose I hang myself?

*Bis.* There I'll leave you.

*Dur.* And a happy riddance: the gallows is welcome.

*Bis.* Hold, hold, sir, [*Catches him by the Arm, going.*] one word before we part.

*Dur.* Let me go, madam,—or I shall think that you're a man, and, perhaps, may examine you.

*Bis.* Stir if you dare; I have still spirits to attend me, and can raise such a muster of fairies, as shall punish you to death.— Come, sir, stand there now, and ogle me: [*He frowns upon her.*] Now a languishing sigh: [*He groans.*] Now run, and take my fan,—faster. [*He runs, and takes it up.*] Now play with it handsomely.

*Dur.* Ay, ay. [*He tears it all in pieces.*

*Bis.* Hold, hold, dear, humorous coxcomb! Captain, spare my fan, and I'll—Why, you rude, inhuman monster! don't you expect to pay for this?

*Dur.* Yes, madam, there's twelve pence; for that is the price on't.

*Bis.* Sir, it cost a guinea.

*Dur.* Well, madam, you shall have the sticks again.

[*Throws them to her, and exit.*

*Bis.* Ha! ha! ha! ridiculous, below my concern! I must follow him, however, to know if he can give me any news of Oriana.[*Exit.*

## SCENE IV.

LAMORCE'S *Lodgings.*

64

*Enter* Young Mirabel.

*Y. Mir.* Bloody hell-hounds! I overheard you:—Was not I two hours ago, the happy, gay, rejoicing Mirabel? How did I plume my hopes in a fair, coming prospect, of a long scene of years! Life courted me with all the charms of vigour, youth, and fortune; and to be torn away from all my promised joys, is more than death;—the manner too, by villains!—O my Oriana, this very moment might have blessed me in thy arms! —and my poor boy! the innocent boy! Confusion!—But hush, they come—I must dissemble still.—No news of my wine, gentlemen?

*Enter the Four* Bravoes.

*1 Bra.* No, sir, I believe your country booby has lost himself, and we can wait no longer for't:—True, sir, you're a pleasant gentleman, but, I suppose you understand our business?

*Y. Mir.* Sir, I may go near to guess at your employments; you, sir, are a lawyer, I presume—you a physician, you a scrivener, and you a stock jobber.——All cut-throats, egad! [*Aside.*

*4 Bra.* Sir, I am a broken officer; I was cashiered at the head of the army, for a coward, so I took up the trade of murder, to retrieve the reputation of my courage.

*3 Bra.* I am a soldier too, and would serve my king; but I don't like the quarrel, and I have more honour than to fight in a bad cause.

*2 Bra.* I was bred a gentleman, and have no estate; but I must have my whore and my bottle, through the prejudice of education.

*1 Bra.* I am a ruffian too; by the prejudice of education, I was born a butcher.—In short, sir, if your wine had come, we might have trifled a little longer.—Come, sir, which sword will you fall by? mine, sir?

| *2 Bra.* Or mine? | [*Draws.* |
| *3 Bra.* Or mine? | [*Draws.* |
| *4 Bra.* Or mine? | [*Draws.* |

*Y. Mir.* I scorn to beg my life; but to be butchered thus!—O, there's the wine!—this moment for [*Knocking.*] my life or death.

Enter ORIANA.

Lost! for ever lost!—Where's the wine, child!     [*Faintly.*

*Oriana.* Coming up, sir. [*Stamps.*

Enter DURETETE with his Sword drawn, and six of the<br>GRAND MUSQUETEERS, with their Pieces presented,<br>the RUFFIANS drop their Swords.—<br>ORIANA goes off.

*Y. Mir.* The wine, the wine, the wine! Youth, pleasure, fortune, days and years, are now my own again! Ah, my dear friends! did not I tell you, this wine would make me merry?—Dear Captain, these gentlemen are the best natured, facetious, witty creatures, that ever you knew.

Enter LAMORCE.

*Lam.* Is the wine come, sir?

*Y. Mir.* O yes, madam, the wine is come——see there! [*Pointing to the* SOLDIERS.] Your ladyship has got a very fine ring upon your finger.

*Lam.* Sir, 'tis at your service.

*Y. Mir.* O ho! is it so? Thou dear seven hundred pound, thou'rt welcome home again, with all my heart!—Ad's my life, madam, you have got the finest built watch there! Tompion's, I presume?

*Lam.* Sir, you may wear it.

*Y. Mir.* O madam, by no means, 'tis too much—Rob you of all!—[*Taking it from her.*] Good, dear time, thou'rt a precious thing, I'm glad I have retrieved thee. [*Putting it up.*] What, my friends neglected all this while! Gentlemen, you'll pardon my complaisance to the lady.—How now! is it civil to be so out of humour at my entertainment, and I so pleased with yours? Captain, you're surprised at all this—but we're in our frolics, you must know.—Some wine here!

Enter SERVANT, with Wine.

Come, Captain, this worthy gentleman's health.

*[Tweaks the First* Bravo *by the Nose; he roars.*

But now, where—where's my dear deliverer, my boy, my charming boy?

*1 Bra.* I hope some of our crew below stairs have dispatched him.

*Y. Mir.* Villain, what say'st thou? dispatched! I'll have ye all tortured, racked, torn to pieces alive, if you have touched my boy.—Here, page! page! page![*Runs out.*

*Dur.* Here, gentlemen, be sure you secure those fellows.

*1 Bra.* Yes, sir, we know you, and your guard will be very civil to us.

*Dur.* Take them to justice. [*The* Guards *carry off the* Bravoes.] Now for you, madam;——He! he! he! I'm so pleased to think that I shall be revenged of one woman, before I die.—Well, Mrs. Snap Dragon, which of these honourable gentlemen is so happy to call you wife?

*1 Bra.* Sir, she should have been mine to-night, 'cause Sampre, here, had her last night.—Sir, she's very true to us all four.

*Enter* Old Mirabel, Dugard, *and* Bisarre.

*Old Mir.* Robin! Robin!—Where's Bob? where's my boy!— What, is this the lady? a pretty creature, 'faith!—Harkye, child, because my son was so civil as to oblige you with a coach, I'll treat you with a cart, indeed I will.

*Dug.* Ay, madam, and you shall have a swinging equipage, three or four thousand footmen at your heels, at least.

*Dur.* No less becomes her quality.

*Bis.* Faugh! the monster!

*Dur.* Monster! ay, you're all a little monstrous, let me tell you.

*Enter* Young Mirabel.

*Old Mir.* Ah, my dear Bob! art thou safe, man?

*Y. Mir.* No, no, sir, I am ruined: the saver of my life is lost!

*Old Mir.* No, he came and brought us the news.

*Y. Mir.* But where is he?

*Enter* ORIANA.

Ha! [*Runs and embraces her.*] My dear preserver! what shall I do to recompense your trust?—Father, friends, gentlemen, behold the youth, that has relieved me from the most ignominious death!—Command me, child; before you all— before my late, so kind, indulgent stars, I swear to grant whate'er you ask.

*Oriana.* To the same stars, indulgent now to me, I will appeal, as to the justice of my claim: I shall demand but what was mine before—the just performance of your contract to Oriana.

[*Discovering herself.*

*Omnes.* Oriana!

*Oriana.* In this disguise I resolved to follow you abroad, counterfeited that letter, that brought me into your service; and so, by this strange turn of fate, I became the instrument of your preservation; few common servants would have had such cunning; my love inspired me with the meaning of your message, because my concern for your safety made me suspect your company.

*Dur.* Mirabel, you're caught.

*Y. Mir.* Caught! I scorn the thought of imposition—Caught! No, 'tis my voluntary act; this was no human stratagem, but by my providential stars, designed to show the dangers wandering youth incurs, by the pursuit of an unlawful love; to plunge me headlong in the snares of vice, and then to free me by the hands of virtue: Here, on my knees, I humbly beg my fair preserver's pardon; my thanks are needless, for myself I owe: And now, for ever, do protest me yours.

*Old Mir.* Tall, all di dall! [*Sings.*] Kiss me, daughter—no, you shall kiss me first, [*To* LAMORCE.] for you're the cause on't. Well, Bisarre, what say you to the captain?

68

*Bis.* I like the beast well enough, but I don't understand his paces so well as to venture him in a strange road.

*Old Mir.* But marriage is so beaten a path, that you can't go wrong.

*Bis.* Ay, 'tis so beaten that the way is spoiled.

*Dur.* There is but one thing should make me thy husband—I could marry thee to-day, for the privilege of beating thee to-morrow.

*Old Mir.* Come, come, you may agree for all this;—Mr. Dugard, are not you pleased with this?

*Dug.* So pleased, that, if I thought it might secure your son's affection to my sister, I would double her fortune.

*Y. Mir.* Fortune! has she not given me mine? my life—estate—my all? and what is more, her virtuous self?—Behold the foil [*Pointing to* Lamorce.] that sets this brightness off! [*To* Oriana.] Here view the pride, [*To* Oriana.] and scandal of the sex!

What liberty can be so tempting there,
[*To* Lamorce.
As a soft, virtuous, am'rous bondage here?
[*To* Oriana.

### THE END.

69

Lightning Source UK Ltd.
Milton Keynes UK
UKHW012029270722
406481UK00002B/52